PRAISE FOR

Tale of the Unlikely Prince

"*Tale of the Unlikely Prince* follows the style and impact of a C.S. Lewis fiction spellbinder for teens and young adults alike. It's also the perfect birthday or holiday gift to both entertain and inspire with eternal truths embedded in a page-turning thriller. Make certain you share this book with every young person you know!" -Dr. Larry Keefauver, Bestselling Author and International Teacher.

"Life Changing Book! Such humor in young adult books is very much appreciated. This book does it very well." Larry Yoder, Publisher's Representative and Developmental Editor.

"*Tale of the Unlikely Prince*, is a fantasy told with great flavor in the age-old art of storytelling. The story promotes life-changing lessons that all young people must face at one time or another. This adventurous epic fantasy will appeal to young adults and even a few older readers as well." Emily-Jane Hills Orford, Author.

Tale of the Unlikely Prince

DR. BILL SENYARD

I would like to especially thank my beloved wife and editor, Eunice. Couldn't do it without you.

No dragons, elves, or gnomes were physically harmed in the writing of this book. A few got their feelings hurt by the alleged negative representations included. It turns out many dragons are very sensitive. Who knew? We regret any discomfort caused by the story.

Also, all dragons appearing in this work are fictitious. Any resemblance to real dragons, living or dead, is purely coincidental.

Contents

1

The Tale of the Unlikely Prince

"There are tales we tell our children when they go to bed," began the storyteller with a wave of her hand, hushing the large audience before her. "Then there are stories we adults read for instruction, fun, and inspiration—motivating us through our hard days. But few true legends not only entertain generation after generation but also shape a people, a culture and even a world. Hear one such account."

The storyteller paused and graciously looked about the room into the engaged eyes of person after person, the tall, the short, the large, the small, the men, women, boys, girls, the well-off and the poor, light-skinned, dark-skinned—all who had gathered for this extraordinary event.

The grand royal stage appeared empty except for the Grande Dame poised on a simple wooden stool. She held a large, ancient-looking book with an ornately carved leather binding spread open on her lap—white gloves on her hands to protect this priceless, historic volume from any harm due to skin oils and such.

She looked elderly, not in some disparaging way at all. Maybe the better word to describe her would be 'grandmotherly' —not tall, a bit full-figured, and finely dressed in a rich black gown with white trimmings. Her silvery hair tied up into a neat bun, highlighted by rich pink bougainvillea flowers woven here and there framing   her rounded and friendly face—endowed with bright eyes and an endearing smile brightening the room.

People have tried to find the right words to describe her. "Special." "One of a kind." "Courageous." "Compassionate." The best adjective capturing her, I think, is "whole." She is who she is— one of the best things to be said about any person.

If you knew her whole story, you would agree she is a miracle—very special. Her dark skin marked by wrinkles and crow's feet, and yes, even scars—bore evidence of a compelling life jam-packed with great stories of her own. I assure you, with more time, each of her adventures would be well worth hearing. But, of course, that will have to be another story for another day.

The Royal Storyteller, Berenice, has arrived. The 'she is who she is' captured the complete attention of this large, expectant audience made up of all the people in the Kingdom, and of course, you as well, to tell the *Tale of the Unlikely Prince*.

She began.

Not so long ago, in a beautiful kingdom not so very far away, lived a glorious King and his troubled, all-too-human son, Yeled. The story is mostly about Yeled, but the tale definitely cannot be told without this king.

Where should we begin? Well, it begins and ends as it should, with the great King.

The King was a very good King, but, like all kings, often misunderstood and sometimes feared by the people. Yet, no King ever loved or provided more for his people. No one was more loved *by* the great King than his adopted son, Prince Yeled. And yet, Yeled, well, let's not jump ahead of the story. First things first.

Yeled was only a boy when he was adopted by the King. The legend is—and we all know legends have some truth—the prince's birth parents were killed in a failed coup. Rebels had conspired to overthrow the great King. I am telling you the truth. I wouldn't kid about something so horrific. It had been completely unsuccessful—a foolish matter altogether.

Truth be told, this wise King and powerful warrior, could never be overthrown by a mere coup of arrogant usurpers.

If you want my opinion, I believe there will be no successful coup—ever.

Since you appear to be interested, let me tell you the actual historical account of events told to me by someone in good authority. The truth is almost always more interesting and bizarre than the *Cliff Note* versions.

The city managers of Garden City (who will forever remain nameless) rebelled against the good King and his rule. Back then, I am told, Garden City was spectacular, lush and green. It lacked for nothing. Today, if you could visit the barren Garden City and her ruined central park—tragically desolate—why would you?

Oh, let's not forget! A shriveled, disappointing tree in the middle of the old, dusty garden remains—another story all on its own. The only other vegetation to speak of are dusty fig bushes lining the outside of the city walls. The word is they are quite void of any fruit. I suppose you could say they serve very little purpose.

I digress.

The coup took place long before there was any wall around Garden City. It didn't need one back then. All were at peace and lacked for nothing. All the people enjoyed intimate fellowship with the King and felt worthy and loved—in a word—enviable, far beyond what they could possibly earn or deserve. This King, the good King, made it so each would feel honored.

One of our court psychiatrists once said, "Everyone needs someone who is irrationally crazy about them." In this kingdom, that someone was the great King. I am not the only one who thinks so.

As strange as it may sound to modern ears, this King didn't demand the glory or hog all sense of well-being. He could have. But, he had a way of spreading it all around, from the young to the old, the well to the infirmed, the tall and short, girl or boy, the educated and non.

One historian of some note recorded these words before the unfortunate uprising. "The people in Garden City experienced honor from the King just like everyone else. They knew no shame, only worth. They didn't need to wear a stitch of clothes as they did their daily routines around the garden."

I can't imagine—but it's a fact. They just weren't concerned with how they looked to other people. No one worried if they were or weren't people of value or whether they were attractive to others. I'll freely admit this sounds like I made it up—but I promise, this was the way it was. I have checked the facts closely.

So, it surprised everyone when it happened. The great rebellion, I mean. No one, including my source, can answer the "why?" question. Why did the two city managers start a tragic, silly, stupid and horrible rebellion against the great King's rule?

Yet the rebellion went on for years.

At one point, the city managers' birth son, Yeled...Oops, did I mention the city managers were husband and wife? Oh, and did I mention Yeled's birth parents were the rebel leaders, long before the King adopted him? Don't worry; I will clear up any confusion as we proceed.

Where was I? Oh, yes. Yeled, a mere 15 summers old, was chosen to mount a cavalry charge right into the heavily fortified center of the King's siege forces—a horrible idea!

If you had a list of the worst cavalry charges of all time, which would have to include Napoleon at Waterloo, the British charge of the Light Brigade, and the Orcs at the siege of Gondor, this Garden City fiasco would still be at the top— epically bad.

Questions still abound. Did they just have bad intelligence? Did young Yeled impulsively act on his own? Did he do it to earn honor or to prove himself a man? It is hard to say. Me? I suspect he did it to make his father proud of him. Boys do such things. Girls too, I suppose.

Why do I come to this conclusion? I am told on good authority, unfortunately, the last thing his dad passive-aggressively said to Yeled before he launched the charge was "Boy, make your mother and me proud <u>this time</u>."

"This time...???" Are you kidding me? No good father would utter such words to an insecure teenager, would they? If this is true, it explains so much. No wonder he was an *unlikely* prince—do you know what I mean?

I digress... again.

Military experts agree Yeled's forces didn't have a chance. Virtually all were lost, including Yeled's parents.

Yeled was captured alive, though wounded and very ashamed. To this day, he still carries the noticeable scar from a saber's slash along his left jawline, from the corner of his mouth to just beneath his sideburns. And you know not all scars are external. He just knew he had disappointed his father so much.

The war-weary "freedom lovers" (as they referred to themselves, ironically) in Garden City immediately initiated negotiations for Yeled's safe return.

[Storyteller's note: Some more fashion-forward residents of Garden City even had t-shirts made that said "Got Eleutheromania?" Eleutheromania refers to the intense and irresistible desire for freedom. Freedom from the good King's rule, I suppose. I believe that it is actually eleutherophobia, a fear of freedom. I will leave it for you to decide.]

Back to my story. Multiple high-level envoys were going from gate to gate—the first shuttle diplomacy. Proposals and counterproposals, yet no agreement was found. Not even close.

Why? Because the King demanded justice. And of course, everybody knows the penalty—the only just penalty for such rebellion—was death. There is no exception to the law of the King.

Well, now things have become very interesting. All seemed lost for Yeled. But then....

Early in the morning, right at sunrise, you won't believe what happened! I still can't believe it. You will have to wait just a little.

2

Sarshalom's Hard Choice

So where was I? Oh yes. The early morning was frigid, February, I think. The skies were still dark and overcast. No moon in the sky for a couple of days and quiet—too quiet.

Then, something strange transpired right in front of the heavily fortified Garden City gate. The guards noticed a single figure approaching under a white flag. Another envoy? A messenger? No one was expected. So, who might this be? As the solitary figure drew close, someone recognized him, the King's first-born son, Sarshalom.

Sarshalom was anything but an 'unlikely' prince. Oh no! He was a great prince, tall, brave and a tested warrior. And like his father, he deeply cared for his people. Everyone loved him—well, except for the people of Garden City, I suppose.

I am not a psychiatrist, so I can't begin to explain what happened next. Maybe the townspeople were so tired and frustrated by the long siege. Maybe they were filled with pent-up rage. Whatever. What happened next was not reasonable. The subsequent scene could only be described as subhuman—in a word, shameful.

As soon as the King's son entered Garden City under a banner of peace, the rebels erupted into an ugly mob. They knocked him to the ground with sticks and rocks and brutally beat him. They brought him before a judge, declared him guilty of war crimes and killed him. The whole horrible thing only took a couple of hours. No one had seen anything like it before or since.

In only a few hours, the great prince, the beloved son of the great king, the sole heir to the whole kingdom—including the Garden City—was no more.

Then, if you think it couldn't get worse—it did! The people of Garden City gathered in the rotted garden in the middle of the city and partied until they could party no more. Can you believe it?

You probably want to know what Sarshalom was thinking. Was this a good idea? Was this his way of honoring his father, the king? Or was this just what great princes do to try to make peace, even at great personal sacrifice?

Other people smarter than me believe the prince didn't act on his own. Maybe the strange plan was birthed out of the great King's war room, in cahoots between the King, Prince Sarshalom and the Royal Steward, of course informed by the counsel of the Royal Vizier, Nomos. One has to wonder if this was the only possible way to finally end hostilities and usher in lasting peace and real glory for both sides? I will leave it for you to decide.

Truth be told, hostilities continue unabated to this very day. So much for lasting peace. But did Sarshalom's death bring any real glory? Well, an excellent question and the very heart and soul of our tale, as you will see.

I truly hope Sarshalom's tragic fate hasn't caused you distress. I had to tell you about Sarshalom because it is part of Yeled's story. You will see why in just a little bit.

Let's quickly move on, shall we?

When the report of Sarshalom's tragic death got to the King, he mourned deeply. You probably know great kings mourn greatly. It's a great king thing. His entire kingdom mourned for forty days. At the end of the time of mourning, the King did something so *unlikely* (I chose this word carefully. Can you guess why?) and yet so magnanimous, it reverberates throughout the land even today. You may be surprised.

The great King formally adopted Yeled—of all people—the erstwhile offspring of the deceased rebellious city managers—to be his only son and unchallenged heir to the entire Kingdom. What?

I know what you are thinking—I am making this up, right? But would I kid about something so mystifying and at the same time, so resplendent? I'm telling you; this is exactly what happened. Unbelievable, but, hey, there it is.

I've spent a lot of time pondering the whole tragic Sarshalom event. Here's the only way I can explain it. While the rebels did the one thing they thought would shame the great King the most, the great King did the one thing he hoped would bring the most honor to the most people of Garden City.

What honor? You ask a lot of great questions. From now until eternity, the bloodlines of the great King and the people of Garden City are forever intertwined. Are you with me? Fascinating, am I right?

Whew, time to take a breath and regroup. I have covered so much, so quickly. Let me step back and give a summary. I don't want to lose anyone. This is too great a story.

Ready? Yeled, the first-born son of the rebellious city managers, is now the adopted son of the great King. He is the sole heir of all the Kingdom. An 'unlikely' prince, to be sure—and so the book's title. Are we good?

What might Yeled be thinking? Let's have some fun. Let's do an interactive survey. You tell me what you think. Just raise your hand. Which of the following statements do you think most reflect what Yeled is thinking as the newly adopted yet *unlikely* prince?

1. I can't believe my good fortune.

2. I feel so loved now by my new father, the King.

3. I really need to make my new father proud of me. I can't be a disappointment to him like I was with my birth father.

Hmmm, very interesting. Thanks for participating. Just looking out over the audience, while I can't exactly count all the votes, clearly, most of you think #1, "I can't believe my good fortune."

We will see. But to mention the obvious, we are just at the beginning of my tale of honor, quests and fellowship. Legends are made of such, and the *Tale of the Unlikely Prince* is an extraordinary legend if I humbly say so myself.

At Prince Yeled's coronation, all came, all bowed low (because bending the knee is what you do, even if you are not totally on board). All did homage to the new royal.

They did so, not because Yeled had done anything to earn it. In fact, the only thing on his resume was the unfortunate cavalry charge which is still studied to this day in the kingdom's military school as an example of how *not* to do a charge.

No, in this kingdom, Prince Yeled's new glory was solely due to the glory of his adoptive father, the great king.

It certainly wasn't based on the name and reputation of his birth parents. That and $5.00 will get you a latte from the castle's barista (tip not included). By the way, my favorite is the double mocha butter candy latte with a little whipped cream. Try it.

I digress again. Thank you for your patience. So much to say in such little time. Back to our unmistakably superb tale.

The people bowed to the new prince because the King proclaimed Yeled's new adoption—some would say 'ascribed' glory. I have come to refer to it as 'so be'd' worth or status. The

King proclaimed, "So be it!" And it was. The unlikely prince is now the *so-be'd* prince. I'll say more.

The final words of the Great King reverberated through the Great Hall and surprised so many, and at the same time, moved many to tears.

"This is my beloved Son, with whom I am well pleased."

...and so Yeled was officially *so-be'd*!

The Royal Sociologist says this practice is common in honor and shame cultures. In most other cultures, your reputation and worthiness are largely based on what you accomplish—what you earn, so to speak. She calls it 'achieved' glory. It is self-explanatory.

If this tale happened in a different place, Prince Yeled would likely be in a probationary period no doubt for a long time. Former rebels would need to prove themselves worthy of any honor. I could tell such a story too, I suppose, but it would not be anywhere near as breathtaking as this one.

In cultures such as ours, glory is mostly *so be'd* by someone of greater glory. Here, the only way to get glory and remove the lingering shame of past mistakes is for the king to share his or her glory with you. The king singlehandedly, for purposes known only to himself, transforms the shamed one into an honored one. Simple, right?

There. Clear for everyone? If this *so-be'd* concept is new to you, no worries—you will pick it up as we proceed.

So, the formerly shamed Yeled immediately became a person of great glory because the Great King said, "So-be-it."

For those of you who are paying attention, this does not mean the unlikely prince *feels* glorious. In fact, for you English majors, who are trying hard to identify the main narrative conflict driving our tale, you need wonder no more.

Yeled is the prince but doesn't feel much like a prince—or at least a worthy prince. In fact, he feels just the opposite. He thinks everyone sees him as a disappointment. It seems his birth father just never got around to telling him how special he was. It seems many young princes and princesses aren't very sure if their fathers—and mothers—are proud of them. It is very sad.

You may be thinking I am being way too hard on Yeled's father. I thought so too when I first heard the story. But the Royal Psychiatrist assures me it doesn't really matter whether his father was a 9 or a 2 on the "good enough parent spectrum." What matters is what Yeled heard. I have come to agree.

Yeled thought about it a lot and constantly worried. "Do all who proclaim me 'prince,' in fact, resent my title?"

He imagined them making jokes behind his back, just expecting him to fall on his face. Why? Like the rest of us, he had a nasty little critical dragonesque voice inside him that never missed an opportunity to remind him of his checkered history.

"Well, you *were* the son of the anti-King rebels. Oh, and you *were* the failed commander of the worst military charge of all time. Oh, and did I mention your adoption cost the life of the very popular Prince Sarshalom, the true firstborn of the Great King?"

But at the top of his self-condemnation list? "You have already failed one father. You will likely disappoint your new dad too."

And so, the title of our tale. Yeled is the 'unlikely' prince.

So, what can he do? In his mind, he must do something grand, something stunning, something truly praiseworthy. What would it be? He will ask the king for a quest—no, a great quest. Oh, this is getting exciting. Are you feeling it too? I wonder if it will work.

3

The Making of a Great Coat of Arms

My inside sources, who claim to be in the know, informed me the King had his greatest craftsmen design a unique glorious coat of arms suitable for a glorious prince.

Reportedly, it took the better part of a month for the right design to be presented to the King. The King was ecstatic with the results. He ordered Prince Yeled to receive no blanket, towel, shorts or robe not embroidered with the new coat of arms. The order covered all cups, plates, saddles and even toothbrushes.

Everyone knows there can be no prince and no real quest without an appropriate coat of arms. And no *great* prince is without a *great* coat of arms. It is the rule of quest storytelling.

This prince had an unequaled coat of arms. Truly, in all the land, before or since, there has not been a more effulgent coat of arms.

[Storyteller's Note: Just making sure we check all the right boxes. All great quest stories must use the word 'effulgent' at least once.]

The coat of arms contained a tri-part royal blue shield beneath a regal rampant lion with a red tongue and fierce claws. The lion stood atop and engaged in crushing a lion-headed dragon beneath his massive paws.

In the upper left third of the shield read the ancient word "*mishpat*" on top of judicial scales. In the upper right the similarly ancient word "*tzedakah*" lay inscribed on top of a red heart. In the bottom third section the phrase "*lipnay melek,*" above a mother gazing into the eyes of her infant completed the unrivaled coat of arms—so exquisite!

What did the strange words mean? Well, I will tell you, just be patient.

As I said, there can be no good quest story without a prince and his coat of arms consisting of mysterious, strange words constructing a bit of a riddle. No good quest story begins with the prince already understanding what his coat of arms means. Fun, right?

But what in the world do those words mean? I will tell you, but you could have just as easily googled it. *Mishpat* is an ancient Hebrew word referring to 'justice.' It's a little different than what we mean by justice today.

Let me see, how can I explain *mishpat*? Think of a time when someone hurt you, treated you poorly, or took something from you. All you wanted was for things to be made whole again. The hurt gone. What was taken brought back to you. *Mishpat* is about making a wronged person right again.

Tzedakah (pronounced tsĕ-dah-kah) is similar and different too. They are often used together. It literally means *right* but is better understood relationally—to *be right* with someone else. You get it, right?

[Sorry, my bad]

If you are right with someone else, you are going to treat them right. So, the *tzedakah* person might see someone who is sick or hurting. They want the person to get well again. They see hunger and want to provide food. They see slaves, and they want them to be free.

Both are great qualities for a prince or princess—am I right? The *tzedakah* thinks of others first, even if it costs them greatly. Remember Sarshalom? There has never been a more '*mishpat*' or '*tzedakah*' royal, ever, and maybe never will be again. He so wanted to make unfair things in the kingdom fair again and to take care of the hurting people, even those in Garden City.

Lastly, the strange ancient Hebrew phrase '*lipnay melek*' is by far the hardest to understand, I think. It is *very* important.

I will give you a clue. It literally means 'in front of the King's nose.' Hmm, not very helpful, I suppose. Well, over the years, it picked up the sense of being *in the presence of the King,* –still a bit confusing and unclear. No worries. Its meaning will be unpacked later, you have my word as the royal storyteller.

Yeled will struggle to figure this one out, and it is the heart of the quest. Maybe we can help him? Don't worry; the quest will unlock all the mysteries.

While I personally love the turn of a good ancient phrase, all storytellers know the importance of clarity. The *Unlikely Prince* is a story for young adults, after all. So instead of repeating *'mishpat,' 'tzedakah,'* and *'lipnay melek,'* let me simplify them. Great princes and princesses should *'make things whole,' 'do right for others'* and *'never leave the King's presence.'* Good rules to live by, to be sure.

Is everyone still on board? Good.

How will the audience know when Yeled finally gets it? Such a silly question. In his quest, the prince will not become smarter, taller, stronger or more handsome. He will not become a better cavalry officer. No, not at all. The quest is successful once the prince not only comes to see the meaning of his coat of arms but, more importantly, is changed in light of the three mysterious riddles. In a real sense, he "becomes" the prince. But he is far from there right now at the beginning of our tale.

Why am I telling you? Reader, I am guessing you have been down a few quests. Everybody knows failed quests have consequences.

So far, this has only been an explanatory introduction. Are you ready to get into the quest? Let's go!

4

The Prince's Problem

So, we spoke about the prince's history and the all-important coat of arms. We also did some very important character development of Yeled—critical for a good story. We used the word 'effulgent' already, and we are only in chapter four. Could it get any better? Oh, yes. We also learned a few mysterious ancient words. Very cool. I think we are ready to get into the actual quest. I can't wait.

We catch up with the prince having an official audience with his father, the great King.

"Father," said the tall, wiry young man. He was not a day over eighteen now, with a head full of long dark hair tied back, emphasizing his broad jaw and—shall we say, more-than-forthright nose. The prince said it very confidently and appropriately, speaking with such a king. He had practiced this speech for some time. It was obvious.

Yet, I will tell you, just beneath his protective surface, he was very anxious. This was a huge moment for Yeled. If the

King refused his request, he didn't know what he would do. He couldn't prove it, but he was still sure others in the court made fun of him behind his back.

He imagined them saying, "Look at him! The usurper boy-prince is the son of rebels. Who does he think he is? We know the truth. He is just an empty showpiece of the King's magnanimous grace, nothing more. Why, he couldn't even make his real father proud of him. Sure, he is *so-be'd,* but he's a disgrace."

Were these real voices or just the paranoid utterings of the unlikely prince's critical inner voice? No judgment. We all have such a nasty dragon inside our brain, a little or a lot. What makes it worse? It sounds like our own voice—or our mothers and fathers. Either way, the voices were painfully real to him. That's the point, isn't it?

"Father," said the prince with an exaggerated conviction. "I request your permission to begin my quest. I have studied under Royal Vizier Nomos for three years now. I believe I have learned all I need to begin my rightful quest. I won't mess this one up. (He emphasized the word 'this'.) I want to finally earn the right to be the prince at last."

Nomos was not only the highly respected Royal Vizier, but he was also the prince's trusted trainer. Since he was *so-be'd,* Yeled could not remember a day without Nomos. Nomos was a short, burly man with an unruly shock of very white hair. He was a bit portly, reminding Yeled of a large garden gnome. His boyish blue eyes lit up when he cracked a joke. But he could also be quite impatient with students. No one treated him lightly, that's for sure.

I would be remiss not to tell you this about Nomos. He was very Scottish, if you know what I mean. He usually wore a thick cotton shift. With each step he took his stiff leather sandals would loudly snap, foreshadowing his presence. On more formal occasions, he would wear a very colorful tartan kilt. Kilts are a kind of skirt for men (but don't let Nomos know I told you). He often donned a red cap. Nomos preferred calling it a Kilmarnock bonnet. Also, his very strong accent required Yeled to request a translation of the numerous sayings he dropped on the young man.

He referred to Yeled once as 'Skinny Malinky Longlegs!' – A tall and skinny person.

Once, Yeled came to class inappropriately attired. Nomos blurted out, "Is the cat deid?" Has the cat died? This means your trousers are too short. I kid you not. Who knew?

For a long time, his teacher intimidated Yeled. But after a while, Yeled began to appreciate his quirky and playful ways. But like I said, Yeled understood no one should ever take Nomos lightly. He was not a man to be trifled with. Not at all.

Once, Yeled dropped a Scottish-ism on the master. It took a bit of research, but he was ready and waiting for just the right time. In one class, Nomos repeated a part about how sneaky some dragons can be in the heat of the chase. This was old news. Yeled raised his hand to get acknowledged and said with a smirk,

"Dinna teach yer Granny tae suck eggs!" Meaning stop teaching someone something they already know.

They both laughed so hard the class could not be continued.

Yeled felt very fortunate to have such a great mentor.

Nomos began to train Yeled in earnest shortly after his adoption three years before. The prince, only fifteen summers at the time, did everything Nomos asked of him and more. Some might suggest he was driven—as if he desperately needed to clear himself of the dark legacy of his birth parents and, of course, the tragic cavalry charge. The truth is, he wanted to make his new father proud—maybe his old father as well.

In one sense, Yeled had it all. And yet, in another sense, he still felt like he didn't belong. "If only they knew my deepest thoughts and fears, they would toss me out on the streets," he said to the mirror one evening. It was totally not true, but to Yeled, nothing could be more real.

To make matters worse, he was living in the former first son's grand bedroom. Can you imagine? He just didn't feel comfortable there. If only he could do something great to finally gain the King's favor and make a name for himself—wouldn't the King feel differently about him then? Wouldn't the people also feel differently about him? He desperately wanted to prove himself to his adoptive father, but he didn't know how.

Then it came to him. He knew exactly what would put him in his father's good graces forever. He needed a quest. No, he needed a great quest—a quest like no other quest. The greatest quest of all time. Maybe then, just maybe, he could rest in his new skin. Maybe then people would forget the past. Maybe he would.

So, he worked hard to prepare. Great quests require even greater preparation. Nomos taught the prince how to do princely things, not just on the battlefield but also in court. Yeled learned the rules of chivalry, civility, honor, faithfulness, loyalty and humility. He learned to fight with a sword, axe, spear, bow and arrow, to ride, joust and wrestle. Under Nomos' tutelage, the prince grew tall and strong, broad-shouldered and confident in his ability to fight. To all appearances, the prince looked like a real prince. All could see his grace, his education, his stature and, of course, his hygiene.

You have probably heard some other princes forsake their monthly baths. Remember, this is real, not just some Disney fantasy.

Princes, no doubt, have their reasons for this unfortunate oversight. It puts the people of the land in a very awkward position, as you can imagine. They definitely notice a prince's hygiene. Who wouldn't? Likewise, who would ever tell a prince to his face he smelled of horse-offing?

In the prince's defense, soaps back then were very caustic and caused red spots in awkward places. No one had thought of adding a quarter of moisturizing cream or manufacturing a floating soap. Such a novelty would seem silly to grizzly soap makers who render pig fat in huge, rusty old iron vats. Fortunately, this prince was careful to make full use of his allotted monthly baths. He was proud of his hygiene.

Shhhh! Can I tell you another little secret about the prince? He had been suffering from horrible nightmares as of late. In his dreams, the King's first son shows up at the palace and retakes his rightful place as the King's true heir. The King lovingly embraces his first son and announces publicly how proud of him he is. Yeled is disgraced and tossed out on the cold, unfriendly streets. The people surround him and throw rotten fruit and goat dung at him, cursing his name—of course in a cockney accent. All quest tale mobs speak old street English. But you probably already knew that.

"Now look at him, the wannabe royal. Just a fake son, a usurper, a deceiver. What were you thinking, boy? Your *so-be'ing was just for show*. Unworthy, unworthy, unworthy!"

Yeled shared the dreams with the Royal Steward. She was so wise in these matters. Yeled always felt safe with her—even more than with Nomos.

This is the first time I mentioned her—but it won't be the last. Take note of this amazing woman. She is a very important character in the prince's ultimate quest. In fact, she holds a very important key to understanding the mysterious coat of arms. Remember? *Mishpat, tzedakah,* and *lipnay melek*? Good on you. Back to the steward.

The Royal Steward was a thin, mature woman of color—not unattractive, Yeled thought to himself. Her face was adorned with wrinkles due to her age. Her almost white hair was tied behind her neck with a thin blue ribbon. She typically wore a brown, rough-textured, woolen robe. A full hood draped over her steely blue eyes. Her small feet were adorned with simple, open sandals. Her entire persona exuded empathy and humility. Simply put, she cared for people. They felt it in her presence. It was quite a gift.

She spent most of her time with Yeled just listening. I would describe it this way. She didn't prattle like some others in the court. The truth is she rarely spoke, and so each of her words felt weighty somehow. And when she did speak, her voice was of the heavens, dulcet and soothing.

It was said her words and tone could make a troll weep. You probably know trolls are very nasty beasts. The Royal Steward would argue they are just tragically misunderstood creatures. Above my pay grade. But I am not going to test it, believe me.

What did she and the prince talk about? She just kept reminding the prince about the unending and unchanging love of his adopted father, the great King, and how much the great King was already proud of him, quest or no quest.

As Yeled described his nightmares, the Royal Steward replied, "Remember, young prince, such are troubling dreams—but only dreams." Her eyebrows were knit together in compassion, concern or both. "Though it is hard to believe, the King adores you as much as he ever adored His first-born son, Sarshalom. No more, no less. He has no regrets. Sorrows? Sure, but no regrets."

"You can do nothing to earn *more* of the King's love," she assured the prince once again. It was obvious to observers Prince Yeled wasn't ready to hear it—not yet anyway. Sometimes princes can be stubborn and self-absorbed, and insecure princes even more so.

"You can't lose even a sliver of the King's love for you," she said emphatically. "He is irrationally crazy about you.

The King's love never hesitates, never pulls back and never stops loving. The great King doesn't know how to abandon or turn his back. He is so proud of you. You need not—you cannot—earn more of his love. It may feel like you need to do something more. I understand and sympathize with you. Yet, you are the King's son. Dwell on your relationship with him. When you are *lipnay melek* (there's the mysterious phrase on the coat of arms) in the presence of your father, make sure you look into his eyes. Then you will know."

"If you want to worry about something, worry about the nasty, critical inner voice inside your head clearly not serving you well. A nasty dragon seems to want you to think you are a disappointment. He will greedily gobble up any thoughts about your worth. Please hear me, prince. Look up into your father's eyes, his measuring gaze. Then these dreams will diminish and perhaps pass—yet not without daily effort on your part, I suspect. Shame's roots go deep."

Unfortunately, the dreams *didn't* pass. In fact, they happened more often. I share these intimate details about the prince with you so you will understand him better. He is not alone. It turns out many princes—and princesses—can relate. Maybe you?

Oh my. I am not so sure he is ready for a quest, are you? Don't you need to have it all together when you face a fierce dragon, or two, or a dozen? One misstep, one little hesitancy, one distraction because you didn't get enough sleep due to some recurring nightmare—and BOOM, you're done!

And we were just beginning to like Prince Yeled. Maybe, just maybe something's at play we are not aware of? I hope so.

Back to the prince.

5

The Official Request

As the fairly hygienic prince stood before the great King, he pointed at the coat of arms on his vest.

"My King, I would test my mettle to prove my worth to you under the most challenging circumstances. How else would I ever know? How else would you ever know, Father?

O great King, you deserve such a princely prince who makes you smile when you consider him, whose reputation brings you glory and honor, about whom you would want to brag: 'This is my son; I am well pleased with him.' I want to be such a prince. Honor me with a quest—nay, an unprecedented quest. I must be sure."

"In short," (it should be noted princes are rarely short with their speeches) "I would like to prove myself worthy of your favor. I would hear you say to me in private and in public, 'Well done, my faithful son.' I would prove to everyone in court I am more than just a foster child, a creation of circumstance, an adopted orphan to whom so much has been given but not deserved. I do not want to be the 'unlikely' prince anymore. I want to deserve the title and to show you, the Royal Steward and Nomos I am worthy. I want to know you love me—yea verily—even *like* me. I promise I will do this in the name and memory of your first-born son."

Yeled paused to catch his breath but realized all were staring, a bit shocked.

"I need to prove my worth to myself as well," he said as he placed his hand over his heart. "I want to see a true prince looking back at me in the mirror. Oh, great King, I beg you. Give me my quest—my great quest. I will do it."

The King stared into the eyes of the young man for what felt like a very long time. There was little emotion on his face—not pleasure, pride, criticism or disappointment—nothing the prince could discern anyway. After a pregnant pause, a royal tear formed in the King's royal eye and ran down his royal face. This King was a very emotional King. His empathy and compassion for all were legendary. The prince's request moved the King. Good or bad? I will leave it for you to speculate.

Finally, the uncomfortable silence ended. The King silently nodded to the prince and began to speak. His words were not just for the prince but for all witnesses throughout the land.

"Let it be known to all," the great King boldly proclaimed as he stood over the kneeling young man. "The prince has requested and will be given a substantial quest—nay, a great quest due a great prince. Yea verily. He will receive a quest worthy of a great king. At the end of said quest, this prince will know (the King emphasized the word 'will' so much no one, except perhaps the prince, missed it)—he will at last know his place in my heart."

The great King's resplendent voice echoed throughout the imposing chamber. The people bowed. A resonating silence followed. It seemed the whole creation paused.

When the prince, who also had bowed his head, opened his eyes, he happened to see the King turn to Nomos and wink.

"Strange," the prince thought to himself. He would have to consider this later.

"Royal Vizier Nomos," the King said directly to Nomos with a smile. "Your work is complete. It would seem your student has learned all he can from you. We trust it has been sufficient for the rigors of a quest. Such a quest will test his mettle, stretch his character and steel his passions."

Nomos bowed to the King. Then he lumbered over to Prince Yeled, stretched up to his very tiptoes and kissed him on both cheeks—a Scottish thing, I suppose. It was an odd sight. Yeled was well over six feet. And Nomos—well, Nomos wasn't even close. "Aye, the air is so much better down 'ere," Nomos joked. No one else thought so.

Nomos whispered something into the prince's ears, just for him to hear. I have it on good authority that he said, "You've got this, my lad. I am already proud of you."

[Storyteller note: Remember how different this was from what his birth father told him before the unfortunate cavalry charge?]

After one more endearing glance, Nomos gave Yeled a broad, toothy grin and exited the great hall, his sandals snapping with each step.

A little secret? Nomos was not surprised at the prince's request. Not in the least. Questing is in the very nature of young princes—and princesses, for that matter. Royals are very human after all and feel they must 'do' in order to 'be'. It was not Nomos' job or his skill mix to disabuse such notions from the minds of insecure young princes or princesses. A quest was in order. You will see what I mean.

"My beloved son," the King said as he looked compassionately at the prince. "All this and every aspect of the quest *will* be accomplished. There *will* be no failure. You *will* find what you are looking for. There *will* be no veering to the right or left, no hesitancy, no disappointment, for any negligence or dereliction at all would be quite consequential. Is this clear? Be aware, this quest involves something far more dangerous, disturbing and unsettling than you can imagine—or be trained for. More than you know right now. There are worse things than the dragons you will come upon out there. Is this also clear?"

"I hear and obey," said the prince, hardly listening now as he was about to explode with excitement. It's a curse of the young, I suppose. No doubt, he was thinking ahead to the many glories waiting for him. Who could blame him? He was going to earn the favor of a father at last, he hoped.

"Prince," the King continued. "This quest *will* be accomplished through many trials and great tribulations. Your experience of your core prince-ness is at hand."

"I also decree the Royal Steward will come alongside of you. She will not carry a sword or spear. She will not intervene in your quest. She will not fight dragons. No. Her role is to be my presence, my heart, my eyes, my ears and to offer you truth and encouragement. She will remind you of my love and how proud of you I am already. You will need this at times. I am sure."

This was the moment Yeled had dreamed about for a long time and was the most frightened of as well. Yeled knew his life would never be the same, nor would he ever be seen the same by others.

"It is all up to me now," he thought to himself. "Am I that prince? Can I do princely? Can I earn the right to be in the presence of the King and expect my father's pleasure and favor in return? Can I make a father of mine proud? My whole future is mine to conquer. I am ready. Let my quest begin."

I don't know about you, I have high expectations for this prince. This is a marvelous tale, wouldn't you agree? It is time.

6

The Great Quest Begins

The excited prince woke up early the next day and put on his serious battle face—no fanfare or pretense. It was time. He was fitted with a linen undershirt and pants. Woolen stockings covered his legs and draped down to his pointed, closed leather boots. On top of the underclothes was a padded gray doublet to prevent the chainmail from chafing him as he rode his royal stallion and fought his enemies. It could be a long journey to get to where the dragons were.

The chainmail was polished and shiny, quite substantial, covering most of his arms and stretching down below his waist. The body armor was covered by an impressive red and black surcoat emblazoned with the official coat of arms.

On his head, he wore a flexible chainmail coif covering his throat, neck and top part of his shoulders. His sword, one the King had given him, was proudly strapped to his side. The prince was indeed ready. He looked very princely, to be sure.

With some difficulty, due to the weight of his armor, he mounted his tall, majestic steed and left the great castle with spirit and his head held high. The crowd cheered.

The King's Royal Steward humbly rode alongside the prince on an old gray donkey, at least as old as she was. They were quite a pair, to be sure.

The prince had worked very hard, more than most princes, to emotionally prepare himself for this moment. He knew what was required of a successful prince—or so he thought. For three years, Nomos taught him the expectations. You remember? Princes are expected to 'make things whole' and 'do the right things for others'. Oh, there was a third item on the coat of arms? Hmmm, what was it? The prince couldn't remember, which was too bad.

More importantly—at least in his head—he knew how to fight, how to ride a horse, how to defeat dragons, gnomes, some emotionally misunderstood trolls and even very large elves. It was not well known, but back then there were some very big and very mean elves. This was no small task.

The prince knew how to travel light. He knew how to set up camp, how to cook on an open fire, how to get fruit stains out of badly soiled carpets and was even quite skilled at origami; some say he was as good as Jeremy Shafer. He didn't expect to need origami, but one never knows.

He definitely missed Nomos more than he imagined he would.

The pair journeyed south toward the rugged hill country where there had been reports of dragons rummaging through sheds at night and even absconding with the odd sheep, pig or bumbleberry pie. The people of the hill country were known for their pies. Dragons are no fools.

But given the choice, dragons would still prefer pigs. It's not just the taste. But hey, who doesn't like bacon? Do you know what's better than bacon? More bacon, of course. I digress.

But there's more to the matter. Sheep's wool can easily get caught between the dragon's back teeth. They don't floss. I will explain in a moment. They hate the feeling of something stuck in between their back molars. I get it.

A couple of days out from the presence of the King, the quest went south, metaphorically. They found a dragon or two or three—in fact, a lot. The region was seething with dragons.

In a period of three days, the prince fought ten dragons. There were a variety of sizes, colors and temperaments. It seemed the practice dragons the prince had fought in the castle were generally smaller, slower and tamer than the ones in the real world. Who knew?

This was going to be harder than he thought. As I prepared to tell this story, I researched dragons a lot. Did you know the name "dragon" comes from the Latin *draconem*, which coincidentally means "dragon?" Not so helpful, am I right? It can also refer to their "deadly glance." It's a bit more interesting, isn't it?

Dragons are universally misunderstood. Most people think they all breathe fire. Actually, very few dragons spew fire. None of the dragons the prince fought did. Fire breathing requires a very high-carbohydrate diet with a great deal of oily fats. Most dragons can't afford such a diet. By far, most of the dragons, at least in this kingdom, didn't breathe fire. They coughed a lot though.

And unfortunately, most of them had very bad breath. Horrible, in fact. It should be of little surprise. Remember the issue with sheep? Dragon arms and fingers cannot support flossing and so food gets stuck between their pointy bicuspids for days or weeks. Yuck!

One such halitosis-affected dragon happened to get very close to the prince's face and breathed out all over him. The horrific smell of the dragon's breath stunned the prince. The effluvia caused the prince to faint. For those who are ill-trained in the English language, 'effluvia' refers to the toxic smell of rancid decaying matter—in a word, "YUCK!" Here's another word: "STINKY!" Or "PEE-YOU!" You get the general idea. It was so bad; the prince had blocked out the event for years. By the time the prince's head cleared, the dragon was long gone. Score one for the dragons.

One very fast and vocal dragon wore a baseball cap backwards on its bulbous green, scaly head. A little-known fact. Dragons were into baseball long before humans. There was an entire dragon baseball league with ten teams, playoffs and sponsors. The Birmingham Yellow Wings were dominant—three championships in five years. Lately though, the London Red Scales have been quite a challenge.

This dragon was apparently a member of the Manchester Funny-Looking Feet. They were at the bottom of the league. One wonders if it has something to do with their name. I will leave it for you to decide.

Why baseball? The dragons attempted soccer. But think about it. Twenty-two dragons running around a grass field—with huge claws—left the pitch shredded and unusable for the next team. And you could always find a huge single dragon to squat in front of the net. Who could score? The usual final score was 0-0. It was not much fun to watch. And don't get me started on the dragon basketball tournament.

Yeled struggled to get his mojo going. He chased one of the slower dragons for a while, but it turned out to be a very large turtle dressed up to look like a dragon. Everyone knows turtles are quite insecure. And let's face it, every reptile wants to be a dragon. They are way cool. The aspiring dragon didn't fool Yeled—well not for very long anyway. Yeled shook his head and laughed at himself as the turtle-dragon slowly crawled away.

Anyway, where was I?

By the end of the third day, the dejected prince was a pitiful, rumpled sight. He could only slump in front of his campfire, licking his many wounds. He took the time to review the play-by-play of the quest so far.

Three of the smaller dragons had bitten and scarred him up quite badly. He didn't expect them to be so fast and so mean. He also got a nagging, tiny little splinter in his right index finger. Of course, splinters are the worst. Am I right?

Fortunately, the Royal Steward knew first aid. She was an accomplished healer and a bit of an expert in the ancient art of splinter removal. Some can do it well, others...not so much.

Still, Yeled was very disappointed in his efforts so far. He had not turned away from the fight, yet it would hardly be called a victory by any measure. He had the external and internal scars to prove it. He didn't want to dwell on it. Five of the larger, slower dragons got away untouched.

Three-day scorecard: Yeled-1, Dragons-9. Nowhere near legendary, for sure. One of the dragons he had vanquished didn't put up much of a struggle. He suspected it was quite old and didn't have the wherewithal to fight back. In the end, the defeated dragon limped back into his comfortable cave using an old, knobby cane, coughing and wheezing the whole way.

Yeled counted this confrontation as a victory—his only one. Pretty sad, really—and questionable according to most quest rules. But who was going to take away this lone semi-highlight from the beat-up Yeled?

Yeled hadn't expected to fail—to fall so abysmally short. He had dreamed of this day for months. This quest was supposed to be about his glory and distinction. He needed to prove to everyone—and himself—that he deserved to be a prince. Yet, even though he had fought to the best of his ability, it wasn't enough—so many things he could have done better, quicker and smarter.

He shook his head in disgust and thought back to his training. He didn't remember. Maybe Nomos never taught him this one important little fact about dragon fighting. Dragons are slimy creatures; everywhere they walk they leave a greasy trail. Who knew?

Well, you can guess what happened. The prince found out the hard way. His first dragon was a nasty, very ill-tempered, albeit small, yellow beast with a red breast. The prince chased it into a narrow glade, disappearing into some thick bushes. Unbeknownst to Yeled, the trail abruptly turned sharp left.

If anyone missed the turn, they would plunge off a massive cliff and drop into a tall waterfall. At the very last minute, the dragon zigged, then zagged and then zigged again—avoiding the cliff and sure death. The prince tried to do the same but stepped upon a large patch of yellowish dragon slime. Not only couldn't he stop, but he also found himself accelerating toward the precipice.

At the last second, he turned and grabbed some willow branches hanging over the falls, stopping his plunge into the churning rocky waters below. It was an impressive athletic move by the prince. Unfortunately, he lost his princely sword in the process. The King had given him the royal sword on his 15th birthday, and he lost it on the very first day of battle. Could it have gone much worse?

It turns out his bravado in the King's court was a bit of an overstatement. He was a pretty good swordsman, yet he found he wasn't as prepared to fight with a spear or club. Everyone knows dragons are notoriously difficult to kill with spears or clubs—not to mention bows and arrows. Their skin is too thick, and their vital organs are too deep.

It had been a very bad three days, to be sure. He wondered to himself how he had failed so quickly and so completely. Certainly, a real prince would have been better prepared and more skilled than a couple of slimy, overgrown lizards. How could he return to the King and regale him with tales of such little success? How would this record make his father proud?

The King's final words kept echoing in his head.

"My son, all this must be accomplished."

[Storyteller's note: The King actually said, 'will be' accomplished—a very different thing, am I right?]

"There must be no failure, no veering to the right or left, no hesitancy and no disappointment. Any negligence or dereliction would be consequential. Is this clear?"

I am no doctor, but I suspect the prince was becoming quite despondent. True, he did not act like a prince of any distinction. He did not feel like one and was riddled with sadness. "The King will be so disappointed in me," Yeled thought to himself.

Some smart individual invented the word 'bleak' just for this situation. The prince was immersed in shame and self-condemnation.

By the way, we all know what shame feels like. When you mess up so often, you begin to think something is wrong with you. You wonder if you are broken somehow. Are you good enough for people to like you or think about you at all? You look in the mirror and wonder if you are strong enough, smart enough, pretty enough, funny enough, likeable enough, thin enough or in Yeled's case, princely enough. 'Not-enoughness' can be a real problem for people like the prince—and you and me, of course. Not-enoughness can make even princes and princesses very sad.

So where was I? Oh yes, of course.

The prince was not in a good space. He did not do princeliness well—not up to his own expectations—and, he thought, not up to the high standards of his King.

"Surely the King will be disappointed, maybe even disgusted with my puny efforts," the prince complained to himself.

"How can I ever look up into the gaze of my father after this total collapse of princeliness? I can't. How can I wear this coat of arms again?"

"Wait," he exclaimed, "the coat of arms, the three things. I've forgotten them. I can still do them—I should do them—and they will make all this mess a success. Let me see...*mishpat*. I am to be about making others' situations whole again. I am to look for injustices needing to be made right. Hmmm. I'm not sure what justice has to do with slaying dragons.

Maybe the next one? *Tzedakah*? Restoring others to rightness, setting prisoners free—that sort of thing. Hmmm. Again, just not a dragon-slaying thing, really. *Lipnay melek*, in the presence of the king? How do I be in two places at the same time? The kingdom is a long way away now. How can I be in the presence of the King out here? What's the point? Maybe these will be made clearer tomorrow."

He could only shake his head in confusion. The wonderful coat of arms was of little help, really. The prince, once filled with confidence, was now just not sure what to do. The quest had not started well—Okay, it was a bust, but maybe tomorrow? He hoped so but wasn't sure.

The next day was even darker and more overcast (apologies for the easy weather metaphor). There was a deep biting chill in the air (second apology, please forgive me).

This was a very good time for the Royal Steward to speak to Yeled. She drew close to him, pulled back her hood, and looked directly into the beat-up prince's eyes.

"Prince, please hear me," the gentle woman implored. "Look into my eyes. Indeed, you have suffered great losses in these early days. You have also worked very hard. My encouragement is for you to remember the King's love for you. He does not love you because you are worthy of his love. His love doesn't require worthiness; it makes you worthy. He can't love you any more than he did when you left for this quest, and he can't and won't love you any less. Remember looking up into his eyes just before you left? Hold on to that. Events change out here. There are successes and failures—often they look and feel the same. But your relationship with the King is forever. He is proud of you, Prince Yeled. Remember."

Unfortunately, the prince stopped listening right after "Please hear me." No judgment from me. I have been there. Your self-focused brain doesn't allow you to hear from anyone else. You are not being rude; you are being human. All the prince could think about was how poor a prince he had been. He had been bullied by a couple of stupid, overgrown reptiles. No disrespect to all the smart dragons out there. I am just reporting what the prince's wounded brain was saying.

Now everyone could clearly see he was not worthy, not enough to be the King's son. All he could think about was the shame he had brought upon his stepfather's name. He had now failed two fathers in only three years. He wondered if it was some sort of kingdom record.

For this astute audience, you may have noticed the prince thought of the great King as his 'stepfather' for the very first time. While accurate, I suspect other emotions are at play here. What do you think?

The now increasingly depressed prince began to worry whether he could ever go home again. It would be too painful to see the disappointment in his father's measuring gaze. His only hope was to press on while clinging to a feather-thin chance of things changing. But even he didn't believe that would happen.

Maybe—just maybe—he could salvage a little of his reputation of doing princely—a little bit anyway. He had to. The quest had lost all joy for him. He looked back over his shoulder in the direction of the castle. He thought he could barely see it just over the horizon through the narrow valley. It seemed so far away now.

He could only walk further away from the *lipnay melek;* the prince's head hung low, his steps heavy. The Royal Steward knew there was nothing she could say—not yet.

Surely, it couldn't get worse. But then....

7

Can It Get Any Worse?

But then it got much worse.

It was getting dark, and so the prince and the Royal Steward pitched their tents in a beautiful, lush glen wedged in between two gently rising slopes. Tall, broad-limbed trees—sycamores, I think—but they could have been large ancient oaks, adorned each rise. I was never good in my botany and dendrology classes. I did pass, though—but just barely.

But enough about me.

There was a bubbling brook filled with cool, clean water running through the middle of the valley. It was a perfect place to settle in and regroup.

How was the prince doing? Not well—not well at all. All the old feelings of failure and disappointment had bubbled up again. It wasn't pretty, but it was very human. This story might just end badly if something doesn't change.

To top it off, there was a lone sign at the edge of the glen—it looked like a warning sign. It read,

"Warning: Beware of the S______."

The bottom row of the sign had been torn off, making its message incomplete and quite unhelpful.

"Beware of what?" The prince barked at no one in particular. He grabbed the sign off the tree and just shook it, taking out his frustration on it. "Snakes? What does the 'S' mean? Snails? See-Saws? Salad? Salamanders? Are you kidding me? Socks, maybe? Sachets? Sack lunches (well, technically two words—my bad)? Sailboats? Sabretooth tigers? Someone's playing a joke on me, right?"

He did add the last one as a joke. Everyone knows sabretooths haven't been seen here for a decade or more.

Then, to make his point, he threw the broken sign onto the ground and stomped on it until it was broken even further. The Royal Steward knew the prince needed to take a step back and breathe, but he wasn't listening. At this point, he couldn't.

This could be a problem. Those of you familiar with epic quest tales, like this one, probably know Rule #5 of great quests is to *never* ignore a warning sign—even a confusing one. Anything could happen.

But the prince had forgotten Rule #5 or planned to ignore it out of spite. Instead, the prince decided he had finally earned a moment to relax. He took off the surcoat with the coat of arms stitched to the breast, then his boots and all the chainmail. It felt good. He had forgotten just how heavy it all was. Now he was down to just his linen tunic and pants and the smelly wool socks as a slight chill entered the early evening air. He leaned back and took a deep breath. It didn't seem to help much.

After a few minutes, his training kicked in and he dutifully got up to gather wood. They would need a large warming fire tonight.

In a short time, he and the Steward were comfortably sitting on logs pulled up near the raging blaze, their palms extended to claim all the warmth they could. Getting the fire together distracted him for a time, but now his mind returned to the mess he made of his day.

"I need to take inventory," he thought to himself. "Real knights take inventory of weaponry." In this case, his armory was quite depleted. If anything happened in the darkness of the night, he couldn't rely on his sword. He had lost it on the first day, remember? But he still had his bow and arrow ready at his side. He could shoot—not as good as he could fight with a sword—but he was more than tolerable. He drew out his bow and got an arrow notched in place, just in case.

Little did he know what was about to happen. Well, you can probably guess, can't you?

Completely exhausted, the prince and the Steward quickly fell asleep by the dwindling fire. In fact, the fire didn't make it halfway through the night. With no light from the fire, the campsite was pitch black. Nights are often pretty dark, of course. The moon may be out, and maybe even stars here and there. But then there are nights like this one where there is no moon and no stars. This was more than dark; this was dark, dark, maybe even darkest dark. You get the idea.

In the bowels of this blinding blackness, the prince and the steward were abruptly awakened by a fierce, high-pitched screeching, maybe a quarter of a kilometer away. It sounded like a crying baby. No, multiple crying babies—dozens, maybe hundreds of them. Neither the prince nor the Steward could see anything beyond a few feet. But what they heard chilled them to the bone. It sounded like a tumult of dark squealing or caterwauling rolling down the valley, coming closer at breakneck speed. It seemed like a wave of sorts but not a flood of water, which has a very distinctly floody sound. It was a roar of pitter-patter, Pitter-Patter, PITTER PATTER—growing in intensity and force—rushing down the glen toward them. Seemingly unstoppable, unhindered and unseen.

The prince realized too late they were in the way of a stampede of some kind—but of what kind? The prince was still half asleep and was now also in shock. He shook his head to remove the cobwebs, and as a precaution, he put an arrow in his bow. He was as ready as he could be. But ready for what?

Well, listeners, it wasn't water or babies. It was spiders—an onslaught of them—that's right, can you believe it? There must have been a million of them, maybe billions of frantic, out-of-control, ugly arachnids. Arachnida (/e'raeknide/) is a class of joint-legged arthropods in the subphylum Chelicerata. Arachnida includes, among others, spiders, scorpions, ticks, mites and vinegarroons—probably more than you wanted to know.

This can't be emphasized enough. The prince really hated spiders! If he were to personally rank the most frightening animals, it would include bees, snakes and bats, but at the very top of the list would be spiders—any spider—even vinegarroons. He automatically shuddered in revulsion. His pulse immediately shot up as his frightened midbrain ignited his fear cycle—cortisol shut down his frontal cortex, the part of his brain where reason dwelt, his mouth dried up and he subconsciously froze in place. He couldn't move, and he couldn't breathe either.

The prince and the steward were caught in a spider stampede. I did some more research; it had been years since the last spider stampede—long before this prince had been born. No one knows what sets them off, but once unleashed, they can destroy miles of farmland and forests. No one knows how to stop them either. They eventually calm down and go about their daily arachnid business—whatever their daily arachnid business may look like. I did not do well in my entomology class either.

But I digress again.

This was a spider stampede like none other in anyone's memory. There were spiders of all sizes, shapes and dispositions. There were fuzzy ones, striped ones, male and female ones (I suppose they had sexes?), loud ones and quiet ones, tall and short ones. There are more than 45,000 known species of spiders, and they were all headed for the prince.

It was something. The huge brown spiders—some three feet wide—were running in a zig-zag pattern. The gray jumping spiders, with thick, hairy legs, would go airborne, gliding as high as a castle turret and then landing with a thump. There were common black spiders too, with their eight bulging eyes, each looking around in a different direction. Very disturbing.

None were more feared than the black giant funnel-web spiders, who had large, red, puffy, pincer-like fangs hanging from their mouths. They had blood-red beady eyes and chompers able to bite small branches in half. Even small ones were known to leave very painful wounds.

Some of these hysterical and deranged beasts weighed over fifty pounds each. They moved low and fast for their size, hugging the ground with thick, black, hairy legs making the horrible, previously unidentified "pitter- patter, pitter- patter" sound.

Some extremely large tree branches were cracking under their weight. This was not good. The spiders came and just kept on coming. They stomped on everything in their path.

The prince did have the wherewithal to pull up his bow and arrow, but then quickly realized his weapon would do little good. No arrow could stop thousands of spiders. He grabbed the steward, threw her to the ground alongside a large log and covered them both with his mail surcoat. It was a heroic act by the prince.

The prince felt their furry, nasty appendages stepping on his head, his shoulders and his legs. They kept on screaming, poking and biting. They left gross drool on every surface they touched—sticky web-like strings of smelly, thick yucky. Some of the fatter ones sat on top of the prince, bounding up and down, poking and prodding. One sniffed and licked at his ears, which he tried to cover with his hands unsuccessfully.

It is hard to describe the sensation as the spider's prickly legs rubbed on the prince's exposed neck. They were hairy <u>and</u> squishy—oh, and there are no words to describe the aroma.

It was a combination of putrid, rank, whiffy, malodorous and foul. Just combine all those adjectives and let them sit in the hot August sun for a few hours, and you're about there. Oh, how he hated spiders.

It was one of the worst experiences of his life. And there was nothing he could do. He was as helpless as he could be. But he would not move off of the steward. He felt responsible for her well-being.

The rampage went on for a long time, likely under an hour, but if you asked the prince, he would have said it went on and on. It was now just about an hour or so before dawn, and the early light was just beginning to layer upon the former dark darkness. The two slowly stood up from the log they hid behind, and they could finally see what happened.

The landscape was stripped bare. The trees had no leaves, and the grass was gone. They felt all over their bodies to see if either was hurt. Fortunately, while they were both covered with disgusting goo and smelled like—well, I just can't say in a polite audience—neither were wounded.

What few supplies they had—including their tents—were no more. Worst of all, the two were covered with yucky webbing, bites and just plain stickiness. The prince's chainmail and boots were also gone. His surcoat, once so regal and glorious, was in tatters. The coat of arms was barely discernible. Oh yes, remember the unhelpful broken sign? The only part left was the mysterious 'S' right at the prince's gooey feet.

"Spiders? Of course, the 'S' on the broken sign. 'Beware of Spiders.' Oh, I really hate spiders." The prince threw his hands in the air, frustrated with everything and disgusted with life itself.

Moments of abject silence passed. The Royal Steward knew to just be quiet.

"Well, we shouldn't stay here in this valley," the prince decided, feeling he should make a princely decision to protect the two of them. "They might come back. We also shouldn't start a fire. Perhaps fires set them off."

He pointed to a couple of large branches up in one of the few remaining trees. "Let's climb and wait until full daybreak."

That is exactly what they did. As he climbed, the prince noted the arachnid stickiness had gotten into his underclothes. Every time he moved an arm or a leg, the gluey substance painfully pulled at his skin and hair. It was so uncomfortable. Have you ever felt so dirty you couldn't think straight? "Toss good hygiene out the window with everything else," he bemoaned. "I can't even clean myself right anymore."

When he finally got to the branch he wanted, he leaned back on the tree and began to pick at all the goo. In short order, he had formed an orange-sized ball of gathered brownish mucilage.

Did you know certain bees go crazy at the smell of spider goo? Not many people do. The prince found out the hard way. It started with one buzzing, then two, and as quick as you can say 'spider goo,' hundreds of goo-crazed bees swarmed the prince. Since it wasn't quite dawn, he couldn't see them clearly, but he could sure hear them and feel their stingers.

He flailed his arms around his head attempting to swat some of them. But he slipped and fell off his high branch, hitting the hard ground and knocking the wind out of him. Still flailing his arms, he got up and ran toward the stream in the middle of the glen. He plunged in headfirst.

Unfortunately, for some unknown reason, the stream's water level had dropped during the spider onslaught. Maybe stampeding spiders get thirsty? Anyway, there was just a shallow trickle of water left surrounding a very embarrassed prince, face down in the mud—his bottom up in the air—swarming with relentless goo-crazy bees. The linen tunic and pants offered little protection.

By the time the bees calmed down, the prince had swollen whelps all over his back, face, arms and rear end—and of course, he was still covered with spider bites, goo and now cold, chilly mud. Yuck, yuck and more yuck.

Later, when the prince had a moment to finally look at his reflection in the water, it was disturbing. It turns out he was quite allergic to bee stings—or maybe spider bites—or both. Whatever the cause, his once-thin face had swollen twice its normal size. He looked like a pot-marked Mr. Potato Head with swollen red eyes.

Fortunately, the Royal Steward knew how to take the medicinal leaves she brought with her and make either a tasteless tea or a stinky poultice—she made both—and several of each. But healing would obviously take some time. The internal healing of the prince would take even longer.

The frustrated prince couldn't believe what had happened. Less than a week ago, he thought he could do just about anything. Now? He was beside himself.

[Storyteller's note: Can anyone tell me what 'beside himself' even means?]

These latest events just confirmed what the prince's critical inner voice was telling him. Even though he did his very best, his best wasn't good enough. Once again, he was another father's disappointment. He wasn't a princely prince. Everyone could see that. Certainly, the great King—who might be kind and even gracious—would have to agree in the end.

His critical inner voice was working overtime. "What were you thinking? You are not a prince. There are so many better choices. The great King deserved so much better."

The Royal Steward did her best to encourage the prince, but nothing helped. The despondent prince just knew the King would be disappointed. He was disappointed in himself.

The prince did imagine one silver lining. "Well, at least the worst is over." After what he'd experienced over the last three days, what more could the quest throw at him? Dragons, spiders, bees—oh my! At least now he can be a not-enough prince in peace.

But once again, he was wrong.

8

The Others

After only a day of recuperation, the prince regained some strength, though he hardly looked well. They decided to press on anyway.

He was a pitiful sight. With disgust, he looked down at his shredded surcoat over his soiled linen tunic and pants. His barely visible coat of arms, covered with spider goo and dirt, caused shame to envelop him.

They were able to purchase some old sandals for the prince from a traveling merchant. They didn't fit quite right, so he moved with a noticeable limp.

Walking south for maybe half a day, the weary travelers came across—drum roll, please—the Others. Their name doesn't cause fear to rise uncontrollably like the mention of other apex predators like grizzly bears, foxes, Godzilla, Bakugan Dragonoid Pyrus, or even Oz's flying monkeys, but in some ways, they are as harmful.

Maybe you have heard of emotional intelligence? EQ is the ability to sympathetically understand others because it's just a good thing to do. If you have a high EQ, you just seem to relieve relational stress around you and defuse conflict.

The 'Others' did just the opposite. Stress thrived in their wake. C'mon, we all have Others in our lives—often in our family. Do you remember the famous shout-out from Charlie Brown's Linus? "I love mankind; it's people I can't stand!!"—that's the Others.

Have you heard the other adage, "Some people are like birds; you help them fly and once they're in the air, they...well you know... on you." That's the Others.

You were probably told as a child, "Sometimes you need to learn to be quiet even when you have a lot to say." No one shared such basic wisdom with the Others.

Are you getting the idea? "It is hard to find a good listener." In the village of the Others, it is impossible.

The Others were self-focused, unsympathetic people who picked fights just because, and they just couldn't get any more inappropriate. The Others aren't burdened with sensitive hearts.

"Look, what have we 'ere?" said one of the larger, more condescending Others in a thick cockney accent with as much contempt as humanly possible.

By the way, most medium-level villains in true Quest tales speak cockney or some other British accent. According to a recent scholarly study of note, over 71.3% do. We will use this practice in our tale. No judgment to nice and respectable Brits.

Back to the prince, who finds himself in a very precarious situation.

The prince guessed the large oppressive hulk was the leader of the Others, if they even have leaders.

"Hmmm, *pretty* coat of arms. Are you a prince of some sort?" The Other said as he pointed his thick finger toward the gooey mess on the prince's chest. The other Others just giggled and chuckled, knowing the fun was about to begin at the expense of these two pitiful-looking visitors.

The prince, despite feeling very unprincely at the moment, didn't back down. He stood up straight (as straight as his cheap flat sandals would allow) and proclaimed, "Aye, sirs and madams, that I am! I am the son of the great King." Even as he said it, he knew he didn't believe it himself. His whole stance deflated noticeably.

"Really? The great King?" said a tall, thin female Other with high poofy hair, emotionally baiting the prince even more. "'E's your father? Does 'e know you are out here wandering around, getting beat up by a couple of *small* dragons?" She emphasized 'small.' "Look, your pretty coat of arms is covered with dragon spit."

"Wait," said two aggressive twin female Others as they each grabbed one of Yeled's arms and pulled them apart to better see the gunked-up coat of arms.

"We love coat of arms riddles…such fun. It's like charades, isn't it, Gracie?" said the louder one. "Oh, no, Eleanor, you don't mean charades; you mean 20 questions, dear."

"Oh yes, of course, 20 questions. How silly of me!" chortled Eleanor. "Okay, Okay, what does *mishpat* mean?"

"Dearie, you have no idea how to play 20 questions, do ye? 'I spy with my little eyes something green.'"

An argument ensued between the two very large twins over which game they should play, all the while Yeled was getting tugged to and fro between them.

Finally, one Other cried out for the twins to cease and desist. He stepped out of the crowd with some confidence; obviously, he was one of the main Others. He was dressed like a cloaked guru of some kind, with beads, sandals, and a long walking stick he waved above his head. Yeled imagined he was a medicine man, priest or something like that.

"Silence! He is the keeper of COA magic."

He was just abbreviating "coat of arms."

"Oh, magic carrier," he continued, facing Yeled, "speak to us the riddle of the COA so we too can be successful and live happily ever after. Proclaim over us, '*mishpat, tzedakah, lipnay melek.*' What does it all mean? We will listen."

"For your information, there is no magic here," the frustrated prince said. "Even if there were magic, I would not be the carrier. See?"

The Other shaman began to run around the front of the crowd, waving his hands in the air and yelling '*Mishpat, tzedakah, lipnay melek*' over and over like it was some magic incantation.

"Shhhh! Here's the secret meaning," the prince added sarcastically. "They mean 'make whole', 'do right for others' and 'be in the presence of the king'." There, no more secrets. You are all officially so-be'd princes and princesses."

"And by the way," he pointed to the gook on the coat of arms, "not dragon spit—it's spider goo you ignorant Others. But how would you know? Spiders only swarm every century or so. They just happened to pick this year—the year of my quest—to do it."

The prince realized he was lecturing Others but couldn't seem to stop. "And as for the dragons I fought, they weren't small. I'd say definitely medium, and they were highly skilled and in very bad moods."

But as he thought about it, he couldn't be sure. How big do dragons get? Nomos hadn't discussed dragon sizes. Do they come in small, medium and large?

"What I mean to say," the prince said, trying to cover his hurt feelings. "Yes, I think I remember there were perhaps *some* medium-sized dragons in the lot, but some big ones too—a couple very big. The bigger ones just got away before I could slay them properly."

Later, the prince would wonder if it was a good idea to defend himself to total strangers, to "Others." Once the spike of brain chemicals wore off, he realized there was nothing to be gained by convincing a single Other how big the dragons were. Convincing them of his enoughness was not part of his quest—that is, until now.

"Ooooh," one of the more overweight Other's swooned. "My, my, King-daddy will be soooo proud. This is your quest? Hey folk! Princie 'ere is on 'is quest."

The Other emphasized the word "quest" with a biting bit of deep mockery. "Yes, his quest. Oh my!" others echoed and shook their heads dismissively.

"Dada," said one tuft-headed young lad. "Dada, what's a quest?"

"Nothing, my boy, absolutely nothing," said a larger Other all too seriously. "Now go back home and do your chores, or yer mom and me will send you on one, and you'll end up looking like 'im."

The boy took one look at Yeled and ran through the crowd yelling, "MOMMY!"

"Hmmm," said the father. "The lad's right. It doesn't look like it is going well fer ya. We have seen other *real* princes, much larger ones, more princely, if you know what I mean, come through these woods."

The scoffing oozed out of the hairy Other.

"They looked...well, more prince-esque, to be sure. It looks like you wrestled with a beehive too. Not a smart idea for a real prince, am I right, boys?" He gibed the pitiful prince.

The other Others agreed and sneered and taunted him under their noticeably ripened breath. It didn't take long for the rest of the Others to pile on more derision, scorn, and mordacity. [I had to look up mordacity myself. It means biting.]

"And 'e's a bit skinny for a prince, don't you think?"

"And such a forthright nose. There could be a couple of princes in that snout."

"He could use a bath too. Didn't the last couple of princes have noticeably better hygiene?"

The prince had enough. He was still the prince after all—for a little while longer anyway. They would respect him, or he would make it so. He grabbed for the special royal sword at his side, only to remember it wasn't there anymore. "Dang, muffed it again," he thought to himself. "Maybe no one noticed?"

But they did.

"Look, 'ere! A prince with no sword. Ooooh, I don't think I have ever seen one of those, certainly not face-to-face," mocked another of the more overweight female Others.

You may remember Yeled losing his sword in the turbulent waters of a deep, raging river on the very first day of the quest—never to be found again. Well, back to the Others.

"Look, a swordless King wannabe," mocked another female Other. "What are you going to do to us, Oh great, sword-challenged prince? Poke your royal finger into our eyes. Beat us up with your sharp wit. Your stinkiness might just make us cry a little. What 'r your thoughts aboot hygiene? This is humiliating. One hopes for a better cut of royalty. Things aren't what they used to be in the Great Castle."

"Look, you buffoons," said Yeled, now frustrated and very angry. He held up his fists in a fighter's stance. Admittedly, he did look silly bouncing around, challenging the Others to a boxing match—one thin, emaciated bee-stung teen against dozens of big, brushy Others. It only made matters worse.

"I don't need a sword," bragged the prince. "Come on, let's go at it—fight like men—and, uh, large women."

The Others laughed and laughed at the pathetic young man.

Can I say one thing? It is likely obvious to you, no doubt, being the clever audience you are, the prince was not thinking princely—not at all. I am not judging. We have all been there. When we are challenged by Others, our brain releases a powerful fight-or-flight chemical making us either want to fight or run.

Oh, and there's more. The same chemical makes us unreasonable for at least three or four hours. It's brain science. No judgment of the prince. In a very short amount of time, he went from being a prince who heroically risked his own well-being to protect the Royal Steward from the horde of nasty spiders to...well this. People. What are you going to do?

Well, as you can guess, the prince's brain went into 'fight' mode. Bad choice. Looking at the sizes of the many Others, flight would have been a far better option. Ah, but remember, the prince was not being logical, not very princely either. He flung himself on the most vocal—and the largest Other.

The fight didn't go well for the prince. It didn't last long either before he was finally knocked to the ground.

The disdainful wisecracks went on and on and on and on. This is what the Others do, and they are good at it. All the prince could do was lay there, naked, under the onslaught of condescending comments.

Eventually, the Others just became bored and went about their day-to-day monotonous lives, looking for someone else they could emotionally beat up.

The prince was left devastated. The Others weren't the only voices telling him he wasn't enough. The critical dragon voice in his head had been saying the very same thing for years.

And now, for the first time, he became aware of something very disturbing. Most of the time, your inner voice is unmemorable and unrecognizable. Most often, it is your own voice. I suppose it is healthy, or at least normal.

Not this time. The prince recognized the dragon's voice in his head as his birth father's. "Boy, make us proud of you *this* time."

"Poppa, I can't," he muttered just before he passed out.

9

The Beginning of the End

Yeled strained to open his eyes. They were dusty and dry, as if he had swum through an old sand dune in the blisteringly hot Sahara Desert without goggles. Kids don't try this at home.

He tried to shake the cobwebs out of his head, but everything hurt—his neck, his arms, and even his earlobes. How do you hurt your earlobes? The prince did. There was also a sharp ache in his left side, and he couldn't breathe very well—maybe a broken rib or two? He had been in a real battle. He just couldn't remember what happened.

Sometimes loss of memory is the result of a big fight. Your brain just covers it up for a while, as it is designed to protect you from being hurt—in this case, the memory of getting hurt.

Don't worry, the prince will be okay. It just takes some care, some time, and lots of liquids and sleep. This was way before Advil was created.

Just before he fell back to sleep, he asked, "Where am I?"—well, actually, just an incomprehensible mumble. It sounded more like "weeerummereyehmmm?" His heavy eyelids leaned shut as he drifted back into a dark, hopefully healing sleep.

The next thing he remembered was waking up again. The room was still dark, except for a single light off to his right side. He realized he wasn't alone. And it wasn't just a light; it was a torch, a blazing torch coming closer and closer and someone with big hands and thin, long fingers holding it.

He tried to determine who or what phantom was hidden behind the flame. He couldn't tell. Maybe one of the Others?

Oh, the Others—he remembered now—the Others and the fight. And how badly he had handled the whole thing.

Fear struck deep in his soul. Not just any fear. Yeled was terrified.

"Who's there?" Yeled croaked out, urgently looking around, trying to see where the threats were. "Tell me. Who are you?" he demanded. "Speak or fight."

"Son..." the voice echoed eerily behind the torch, sounding more like a slow, wraithlike moan. "Son," it slowly repeated, "make me proud...*this* time...*this* time. Don't be a disappointment again. Do you hear me, boy?"

"Poppa. Da', is it you?" Yeled couldn't believe it. It was his dad's words, but not his voice, and his dad had perished in the coup years ago.

"Why didn't you make me proud, boy?" The specter continued, not in response to Yeled's question and showing no interest in what Yeled had to say. "It's all *your* fault. Do you hear me, boy? You shamed me. You will never belong...ever."

Yeled's stomach felt nauseous. Sweat beaded on his cold forehead. He was having a panic attack. He couldn't move. He grabbed a few quick breaths, but it didn't help.

He was confused, frightened, and struggled to slow his breathing when another voice erupted—not a voice but a screeching. "You don't deserve to be a prince, do ya'? You know, don't you?" howled a vile female character with a thick, unpolished brogue, standing just off to the left of the torch holder. She was moving slowly toward him, only a couple of feet away now.

"Yer a fake. That's what you are," said a little child's voice to the right of the flame.

"Everyone knows your *dark* secret," screeched a guttural voice, emphasizing the word "dark." Someone cackled just behind them. "Yer foolin' no one. Everyone can see what you see."

Now all the entities were moving closer, surrounding him. He could do nothing to stop them. He was drowning in the vile swamp of downward gazes. The creatures began to swirl in the air about him, berating him with more and more accusations.

"It is the King who is the most embarrassed," said the voice holding the bright torch. "He stood up for you. And just look at you now! We all deserve so much better than you. You know who you are," the voice paused. "You're your father's son."

Then, as if on cue, the light shifted, and he could at last see their faces. He blinked desperately, trying to make sense of it all. It was the Others, and they were striking the ground with their pitchforks, axes, and hoes, thumping in a loud, eerie rhythm, bang, bang, bang. In between the striking, the vile crowd in unison cried out, "Fake!"

Bang... "Fake!"

Bang... "Fake!"

Bang... "Fake!"

The light shifted again, and what he saw took his breath away—not the faces of Others. All the men, women, boys, and girls, each to a person, had *his* face—hundreds of Yeleds staring back at him!

He tumbled to the ground on all fours and wept uncontrollably.

10

The Beguiler

When the prince awoke again, he was back in bed—though definitely not his own. His head was still pounding, and though his wounds were dressed, his whole body still ached beyond words. It took a few moments for him to begin to regain the use of his mental faculties, no doubt due to the complete beating he took at the hands of the Others.

He remembered, and it caused shame to boil up again. He should have known better. A true prince would not have let the Others get under his skin. Once more, Yeled proved to the entire world he just wasn't prince enough—certainly not worthy of the King's respect and honor. What in the world is he going to say to the King when he sees him? Or Nomos?

He uttered a deep, deep sigh—you know the kind—it's what someone naturally does who is just totally defeated and can't see a way forward. He breathed in and exhaled again, still not feeling even a little bit better. He could only lift his head—gently, oh, so gently. He had never felt so much pain.

The prince considered getting up out of bed, gently setting one leg on the floor and then the other but thought better of it after he felt shooting pain down his side and even more dizziness. He decided the wise thing was to just lie there for a while, maybe a few minutes until he felt he could manage life again. Maybe the Steward will show up with some of the special tonic she kept with her for such aches and pains. She was quite skilled and her tonics were very effective.

"Wait a minute, the Steward," he thought to himself. "Where might she be?" He realized she was nowhere to be seen. Wherever he was, he was alone. Even more curious, he thought.

Then, like a nasty, painful retching, the memories of the nightmare boiled into his brain, causing him to shudder again. You know, sometimes you have dreams, and upon waking, you can't remember what happened at all. They just disappear into the darkness like a mist. Not this time. Sometimes nightmares can be good, but most are not.

[Storyteller note: I have this nightmare of being chased around my house by a purple dog with no teeth and very bad breath. Yuck.]

I digress once more.

The prince wished he could just forget the nightmare, yet he seemed to recall every ugly detail: the mysterious floating torch, the Others, his father's hands and everyone's face morphing into his own—or maybe they were always his.

Even though his brain said it wasn't real—it couldn't be real, right? It still caused him to recoil with deep apprehension.

He paused and thought, "Maybe it was real." After all, everything was such a jumble in his head. How could he be sure of what's real and what's not? If he was going mad, how would he even know? Don't insane people truly think they are rational? In psychiatric hospitals all over the kingdom, you can find people who are 100% sure they are Joan of Arc, Moses, or a duck. And they are totally at peace with their 'truth.'

These dangerous thoughts made Yeled convulse violently, but since he hadn't eaten for a long time, he just became more and more nauseous. "Oh, where was the Steward?" he thought.

"Enough!" he said aloud to no one at all. Even if it hurt, he didn't want to just keep lying there, having the nightmare keep bouncing around his skull over and over. He needed to do something, even if he didn't feel like it. But what?

He paused and looked around the huge bedroom. In front of him was an ornate picture window, maybe fifteen feet high. Halfway up the sky, a fuzzy, pale orb was trying to burn its way through the thick fog blanketing the valley. "The sun will soon burn through the shadowy vale, and I hope it will warm things up," Yeled imagined.

Little did he know this particular valley remained quite dark most of the time.

Even so, the view of the sun attempting to rise gave him a moment of hope and familiarity. His stomach relaxed a little, and the nightmare's vile fingers released their stranglehold on him for now.

Yeled decided to take advantage of the respite and at least visually explore his surroundings.

The bed he was lying in was magnificent, quite plush, not your typical straw-filled variety he was used to at the castle. This luxurious four-poster bed exuded an air of opulence, royalty and comfort. The bed frame was massive, crafted from rich, dark wood adorned with intricate carvings. The four tall posts rose from each corner of the bed, reaching towards the high ceiling, embellished with lovely decorative finial caps.

Yeled had never seen anything close to this extravagance, even in the highest chambers of the King's palace.

As a matter of fact, this bed was worthy of a king—no, a great king. The headboard and footboard were generously padded and upholstered in sumptuous fabrics; it looked like velvet, silk, or some combination, featuring intricate embroidery of knights and other warriors defeating dragons of all kinds.

"Where in the world am I?" thought Yeled again as he quietly gazed about the spacious bedroom. "Whose house could this be? Or palace?"

Though he wanted to get up and explore some more, he still couldn't get out of bed—not just yet. "Maybe if I just lay down for a few more minutes." So he gently placed his throbbing head on the pillow. And instantly, his life was changed.

Well, it's a bit of an overstatement sent, but the pillow. Look, the prince has slept in a variety of beds, for sure, but nothing matched the dramatic softness he felt when his tired head lay down on this pillow. Most people in the Kingdom had straw-filled beds. They weren't comfortable, particularly the pillows, but hey, straw was readily available. If you had a little savings, you might upgrade to horsehair pillows and mattresses. They are comfortable too, I suppose.

You know, I have always wanted to ask someone where they get all the horsehair. I will have to do some scholarly research and get back to you.

Some of the highest echelon of sleepers prefer down feathers from ducks or geese, but it costs an arm and a leg to get fifty pounds of feathers. Comfortable? Oh yes, you might be surprised.

But this pillow? This pillow was far superior to all of those. Yeled couldn't even find the words to describe what he was experiencing—a "feathery haven of comfort." "Utter bliss to touch and squeeze." It was "so sculptable and, yes, huggable even." Did you know high-end manufacturers measure the moldability of luxury pillows? Moldability refers to how easily the pillow can be shaped or scrunched. The prince's head now rested on a very moldable pillow. It clearly was not manufactured by some machine, no. It was hand-fluffed by someone who knew what hand-fluffing was all about. And of course, the pillow was naturally hypoallergenic. Can a pillow be euphoric? If so, this one was. Yes, surely the best pillow he'd ever experienced.

"What is going on?" he asked himself again as he scrunched the pillow for the fourth time. "Did the King's bed feel like this?" Yeled wondered, still quite distracted.

It was not just the pillow. The prince also noted the bed had a massive canopy made up of sheer and flowing fabrics, creating a warm and dreamy ambiance. The room was also amply provided with expensive complementary furniture pieces, nightstands, dressers, and seating arrangements mirroring the bed's opulence.

And that's not all; his tattered princely clothes, each embroidered with the coat of arms, were noticeably missing. But he was wearing an exquisite, brushed wool nightshirt. Very comfy. It was the most comfortable nightshirt he had ever known.

All this opulence only raised the prince's curiosity. Pain or no pain, he needed answers. "Hello? Hello?" The prince tried to vocalize, but it only came out as a gravelly whisper. "Hello, where am I?" his voice croaked inaudibly.

He tried to speak louder, but his voice was still frustratingly weak.

After some more time struggling to get someone's attention, he heard a sound from what he assumed was a hallway outside his closed door. Steps were coming his way, not in a rush or in any way threatening. Just someone casually coming down the hall.

His door slowly cracked open, and an older man, about the King's age, the prince estimated, stuck his well-coifed, gray-bearded head in the door opening. He smiled broadly and comfortingly and began speaking to the prince.

"Oh, say hello there, young prince. May I come in?" The older man inquired with an upper-class British accent, likely from Surrey or Buckinghamshire. The prince nodded cautiously but did not try to get up from the bed again.

"Welcome to my home. My name is Dolos. I am the lord of this castle. I imagine you have a lot of questions. In time, all will be answered. First, I want you to feel safe. You are under my protection and enjoy my hospitality. Fortunately, I was out hunting by the road this afternoon. I heard a ruckus and saw the Others shamefully beating the tar out of you. I think you were very brave, yet, I must say, the fight was ill-advised even for someone of your stature and skill. I chased them off with my bow and arrows and brought you here. Only as I began to dress your wounds, did I recognize you as the prince. Welcome to my fiefdom, my prince. What is mine is yours." Dolos bowed respectfully.

The respectful bow felt really good to the prince, especially after the cheeky and discourteous treatment he had received from the Others, not to mention the dragons and the spiders. It felt almost as wonderful and scrunchable as the pillow. The prince smiled a little. He couldn't remember when he had smiled last.

"Please tell me, O great prince, why are you so far from the King's castle? These are dangerous woods. I don't mean anything by my comment; it's nothing derogatory. I mean, well, a great prince like you should be leading a great army, a great consort made up of great warriors mirroring his bravery and glory."

The prince thought about it a bit and agreed. Lord Dolos' logic did make a lot of sense. What was he really doing out here?

"The truth?" confessed the prince matter-of-factly. "I was on my official quest, Lord Dolos. I went out from the castle to earn the glory you speak of. Yet I failed miserably, again and again. I have concluded that no matter how hard I try, I am not a great prince, not at all."

As he spoke, the prince, ignoring the constant pain, carefully rolled up to a sitting position on the luxurious bed and planted his naked feet gently on the exotic hardwood floor—maybe rare Zebra wood, he thought.

He was a pitiful sight, really, so filled with shame and self-contempt. He wouldn't, no, he couldn't look into the gracious eyes of his host.

"Oh, young prince, may it never be so," said Dolos as he walked around to stand right in front of the prince, making sure to look directly into the prince's eyes. "You *are* a prince! I have gazed upon your coat of arms. That is enough for all to see you as a person to whom honor is due. Those men and women in the village should never have treated you so. They are a horrible lot. Why, I am surprised—please do not take offense at my words—your stepfather allowed you to go out alone, without an armed escort worthy of your rank."

Yeled was still too confused and in such pain to realize Dolos had spoken of his stepfather, the King. If Yeled were at the top of his game, he might have realized there is more to Dolos than meets the eye. How could a stranger possibly know about his relationship with the King? But Yeled was far from the top of his game.

"Please, young friend, rest up," Dolos continued graciously with a wide, disarming smile. "Later tonight, we will have a feast for you—a grand banquet worthy of a prince of real substance and glory. I will send you a servant. He was my son's servant before my sole heir's untimely death a few years ago."

Dolos clearly struggled to speak of his late son as he paused to wipe a tear from his eyes. It is painful to lose a child, no doubt. Or was it something else? You decide.

"My servant, Momos," said Dolos as he pointed to a man standing at the door. Bald, thin, and standing quite erect, Momos was dressed in a black formal suit with very little expression on his face. "He will serve you well. You can trust him."

Yeled just couldn't believe his fortune finally. No dragons, spiders, bees, or even Others. He just wasn't used to being treated so well. And yet, something was bothering Yeled.

"Excuse me, sir, uh, Lord Dolos," Yeled quietly inquired. "I was traveling with a companion, a woman. Is she here as well? Have you seen her?"

"Ah yes, she was here, of course, and was taking good care of you for a time. She wanted me to tell you she has gone back to the castle for some special medicines, fresh clothes, and other assorted sundries. She said not to worry. She will be back as soon as she can. I even gave her a fast horse and an escort, just to make sure she was safe. But she strikes me as someone who can take care of herself, eh?"

This surprised Yeled a little. Until this moment, he would have never thought the Royal Steward would leave him for any reason. Her charge, which she was very faithful to, was to support him in his quest. But maybe it makes sense. She is coming back after all. He could use fresh clothes, he supposed.

"Thank you, Lord Dolos, for your care and generosity," said Yeled as he attempted to stand once more, his head still pounding. "I am sure all is well."

"Please lay back down, son," said Dolos as he reached out and grabbed Yeled's shoulders for support. "You are in no shape to get out of bed yet. Allow my faithful servant, Momos, to fix you a tonic for your headache and bruised ribs. He is a miracle worker, to be sure."

Yeled did just that.

Are your red flags going up too?

Maybe I can offer you a free trip to an inclusive resort in Cancun—no strings attached? Or scenic swampland in Louisiana for just a handful of dollars. Or the good news that a total stranger in a distant land has passed away and left you as the recipient of his entire estate.

As one wise guy once said, "If a story sounds too good to be true, it's probably sold out."

11

The Shocking Question

At dinner, Yeled got to know more about his host. Dolos was a substantial man, a very wealthy farmer, with cattle beyond count, even a small army at his disposal, and fields farmed by innumerable servants. Not as great as the prince's stepfather, to be sure; however, Dolos' stature was on the larger side of expansive nonetheless.

Over the next few days, the prince began to heal—outwardly, of course, but more notably, inwardly—or so it seemed to him. His host was more than gracious. All that belonged to him and his late son was indeed laid before the prince. They dined, drank, and smoked pipes together. Kids don't try this at home; it is a filthy habit. Yeled will regret it, to be sure.

They told each other great stories—some real, some, shall we say, embellished—and laughed until the prince could laugh no more. Dolos truly seemed to relish Yeled's stories about the dragons and spiders he encountered. Dolos hated bees just about as much as Yeled; in fact, they seemed to have a great deal in common. Dolos never made fun of Yeled's failures, never sought to give advice, nor even showed judgment.

"Brave prince," affirmed Dolos. "It is to your great credit you survived the spider stampede. How horrible! I know of no one else who has. And you risked your own well-being by throwing your body on top of your companion. That was a purely heroic act few would attempt. She is alive because of you, no doubt. You are probably too humble to say so, but I will. You are a hero."

This felt very different from the response he expected from the King. Yeled was beginning to feel valued, appreciated and even respected. So, it didn't take long for him to open up even more about his family in Garden City, the tragic calvary charge, and the so-be'd adoption to the King.

"Ah," said Dolos, making a sweeping gesture with his hand. "I am very familiar with Garden City. I remember at one point in time, the garden there was very lush and wonderful—until it all came crashing down—not anyone's fault really. It is all too bad and highly preventable, uh...at least what I heard."

"Son, I am also so sorry about the calvary charge. But you were only 15, and you were doing the will of your parents. It's not your fault, don't you see? You were dealt a very bad hand. I am sure your father didn't really mean what he said: 'Son, make us proud of you *this* time.' Heat of the moment stuff, I suspect. Do you miss them?"

The question took Yeled aback, and he had to think before he answered. Did he miss his mother and father? No one had asked him such a thing before. All he knew was he had been such a disappointment to them. So, did he miss them? He would say he wished he could go back and do it all over again—better—so he could finally hear his father praise him and brag to his friends about his exploits and character. That is the deepest desire of his wounded heart, even to this day. But it will never be.

Dolos listened to Yeled's story with seemingly great interest and even greater empathy. "My boy, I have no doubt your father was proud of you. I would be if I were your father."

That last statement shocked Yeled, but he was not sure why. I will tell you it was a foreshadow of things to come.

"Have I told you about my son?" Dolos asked Yeled. "He would be about your age. I loved him so much—more than you can imagine. I have no doubt you would be besties with him. He was fun, smart, courageous, competitive and compassionate. Every day, I told him what I thought of him. 'Son, I just want to tell you how proud I am to be your father. I can't wait to see the man you are going to become and what you will accomplish. I would buy stock in you. There is nothing you could ever do to make me ashamed to be your father.'"

Yeled couldn't believe his ears. Did such a father-son relationship exist? Really? Why had he been dealt such a bad hand? It was like he got a 7-2 off-suit Texas Hold'em poker hand. No one wins with such a bad hand, no matter how you play it. While you can bluff in playing cards, it is much harder in real relationships.

Yeled had to admit to himself he was a bit jealous of the relationship Dolos had with his late son—no, he was *very* jealous. That is all he ever wanted. So much more than the quest even.

Lord Dolos's wife, Apatê, was also more than kind. She sewed the Prince's torn clothes and presented them to him as almost new. She even polished his great shield. It shone like the sun. He thanked her profusely and put them both away in the old pine bureau in the corner of their deceased son's room. He wasn't sure he would need them anymore.

Yeled felt quite—what's the right word?—venerated here. Loved, accepted, honored and secure. And, by the way, the scrunchable superior pillow didn't hurt.

A few weeks passed. Yeled couldn't believe he had been there so long already and missed the King less and less. Thoughts about the quest were rarer still. One evening, at dinner, Dolos popped the question to Yeled.

"My son," began Dolos. Yeled had resisted the compliment those times Lord Dolos accidentally called him "my son." But no longer. He actually longed to hear it.

"I have no right to ask you this, so please do not be offended in any way. I am a lonely man with a vast empty house and no heir. Apatê and I just can't stop talking about how well you fit into our household, or dare I say, our family. It is as if my late son has come home."

"And your friend has not returned for you. I can keep sending scouts to find some answers, but you may not want to hear them. You yourself said if you ever returned to the castle, you would be facing only shame and contempt. I couldn't bear such shame for you. You don't deserve it."

"And listen, the impossible quest your stepfather gave you was too much. Inevitably, you would fall short—anyone would. In fact, you did everything you could possibly do—and yet, what are the chances your former stepfather would ever give you your rightful due? In his presence, you just aren't enough, for some reason. You deserve so much more, my son. May I speak openly? You should not even need a quest to prove your worth to anyone. All can see it. I can see it. Apatê sees it. I am rambling." Dolos paused as if to gather his thoughts. "Look, would you consider becoming *my* son? I can't imagine a greater honor than becoming your stepfather. What do you say?"

Certainly, boys and girls, you can see through my gimmick of narrative parallelism. Two adoptions, two sons, two stepfathers—similar in some ways but far different in others. Let me elaborate. In the first instance, the unlikely prince was adopted by fiat into the family of the great King pending a successful quest (or so Yeled thought). In the second case, the failed prince is now being offered a "new and better" adoption—sans-quest. Interesting?

Well, the prince was surprised at the unexpected offer. No judgment from me. I get it. But surely, you've heard the old adage, "If it's too good to believe, it likely is." Are you noticing something non-kosher here? Hold on to those thoughts.

Yeled wondered to himself. "Is it true? Finally, a father who actually adores me, who sees my true potential, who understands what I have gone through, who has my back? This is the favor of a father I have longed for—my whole life—and no need for a nasty quest to earn it? Is this even possible?"

Alas, the prince didn't take very long at all to consider the offer. Why delay? He couldn't recall ever being happier. Dolos was the father he never had—and always longed for. Was this what being a son was supposed to feel like? Lord Dolos never criticized Yeled and never showed disappointment. If he were honest, Yeled had come to prefer Dolos over his stepfather, the Great King—though out of residual respect for his former liege, he would never say that out loud.

The way Yeled figured it, if he agreed to Dolos' request and became his son, this would put this regretful quest to bed for good. "Good riddance," Yeled thought. He had messed up the quest big time. He had not acted princely—not enough, to be sure. Also, if he accepted, he would never have to face the King's disappointment. Or Nomos'. Both would hurt way too much.

It's funny how our minds will play tricks on us. The prince remembers his former stepfather saying, "This quest will bring to you an experience of the favor you long for, dear prince." Of course, you and I know the King didn't say this—not even close. Memory can be a squirrelly thing, skilled at morphing if need be. Such was the case here. We are all experienced justifiers of our own actions. This proficiency is not limited to princes. In the prince's mind, Dolos' love for him was the real deal. It required no quest, no hoops to jump through, nothing more. The prince could be himself at last. That made him smile.

The prince agreed to become Dolos' son and wanted to do it as soon as possible.

To make things even sketchier, Yeled even justified *not* sending a messenger to the King informing him of his decision and the quest's ignominious end. "After all," he made the case in his head: "The King is a long way from here, and what has he done to come find me? Nothing. I am doing him a favor really. Why cause the King more concern and disappointment? What is over is over."

But is it?

12

Not Always What They Appear

At last, the great adoption day arrived. No expense was spared, an affair filled with a great deal of pomp and circumstance. People came from all over the valley. There was laughter, singing and other revelry I will not go into right now. Suffice it to say, everyone was having a grand time. Even Yeled.

Apatê had altered their son's royal garment to fit Yeled. Yeled was about the same size in the shoulders and the waist but was four inches taller. She had done a very professional job.

At the appointed time, Yeled stood before the grand thrones of Lord Dolos and Lady Apatê and kneeled.

Dolos stood over the humble prince and waved his hands over the vast audience, proclaiming, "Today, my son has been restored. Of course, not him, but in the guise of another great knight, Prince Yeled.

The crowd cheered, "Huzzah, huzzah, huzzah for Lord Dolos and His new son Yeled."

Once more, Dolos waved his arms to silence the crowd. To commemorate this event, Apatê had gone to great expense to restore Yeled's great sword which had fallen into disrepair during his quest. He turned to Apatê, took the huge sword from her, and walked back over to Yeled.

"My new son, it is my great privilege to knight you, Sir Yeled." He dipped the shining sword onto Yeled's right shoulder and began to switch to his left.

But something struck Yeled like lightning. "Wait a minute," he said with great concern in his voice as Dolos was lowering the sword to Yeled's other shoulder.

"What is this? My sword? It cannot be. *My* sword was lost on the first day of my quest. It fell into the rapids and could never be found. What is this? What is happening? Wait..."

In a millisecond, to Yeled's shock, everything changed; the entire celebration just seemed to melt away into black nothingness. The crowd was violently absorbed into a dark void, along with the castle and all the rest of the pomp and splendor. Now it was just Yeled, all alone with Dolos and Apatê. Finally, he could see they were also not what they appeared to be.

Surrounded by other-worldly shadows, Yeled watched helplessly as Dolos morphed into a horrible, bent-over, aged man with long, stringy red hair and a severe, hoary face. His eyes lost all their light and were surrounded by sinister dark scars making his mishappened forehead even more disturbing. He seemed to grow to twice his usual size, and now Yeled could see his face was encompassed by a multitude of repulsive black serpents with poisonous mouths bared.

Then, as fast as a snake strike, Dolos' pale hand shot out and grabbed Yeled's exposed neck. His inflamed, contorted fingers, much stronger than Yeled imagined, instantly wrapped around his neck and started to choke him. With surprisingly little effort, Dolos lifted Yeled off the ground. All Yeled could do was flail around impotently, hopelessly trying to pry open the steely death grip.

"You foolish boy," said Dolos with an ugly sneer, drawing as close as he could to Yeled's reddening face, his voice oozing with cruelty. "There truly is no place for someone like you who was given so much and appreciated it so little. What the King..." Dolos said, spitting on the ground as if he couldn't bear to say the epithet. "What he sees in you, I cannot imagine. Before I take what pathetic shred of life you have away from you, let me introduce myself. I am Dolos, the son of my father, Darkness. I am known by other names, such as Mendacius and the Lord of trickery, falsehood, and lies.

My brothers and sisters, you might also know quite well: Fear, Envy, Anger, Unfaithfulness and Complaint. I told you I was familiar with Garden City. I will add I was intimately—if I may say so—familiar with your pathetic parents too. They, like you, despised the gifts given to them and just couldn't stop longing for more. Deceiving them was far too easy.

And you? You *wanted* to be deceived. Like they say, the tree doesn't grow far from the apple, if you understand my meaning.

"Boy!" Dolos now growled like some feral animal, his eyes turning ugly yellow. "Do you want to hear a little joke?" He laughed derisively. "It turns out you are *just* like your father.

It's the definition of irony, of course. In the end, he was not one to count on. He thought so little of everyone. He was never satisfied with the status quo. Always blaming others for his misfortunes. Your mother, too. True, they had their own issues. I will tell you a little secret. They were so easy to manipulate. Oh, and they loved pillows too."

Dolos continued to squeeze Yeled's frail neck harder and harder. Yeled's brain screamed at the beginning pangs of oxygen deprivation. His eyes rolled back in his head. In the end, all he could hear was the vile victory laughter of Dolos and the ugly cackling of his hateful bride, Apatê.

"Enough, foul imp," a voice familiar to Yeled rang out in the din. The voice was very loud and without any inkling of fear. "Release him...or else, Serpent. You have *no* authority to harm him. This one is of the King."

Dolos, caught unaware by the unexpected challenge, looked around to see the source. He recognized her immediately, of course. This wasn't the first time they had tangled. Though he would never show it or admit it, he couldn't help but tremble in fear.

Standing behind him, and about a foot shorter, was a thin, erect black woman, her gray hair wildly unfurled, and her hands raised aggressively into the skies. It was the Royal Steward. Yeled was totally shocked at her appearance. Gone were the warm, compassionate eyes and gentle smile. Her face was filled with rage—the countenance of a great warrior. She stood in Dolos' face as one with unimaginable authority, and Dolos knew it.

Whatever his game, it was over.

Realizing the battlefield had shifted, Dolos begrudgingly set Yeled on the ground, though his age-spotted cold fingers still held firm on Yeled's neck.

"Noomai, you are too late. He is mine." Dolos barked at her with great contempt, though perhaps some apprehension as well. When such evil is faced with a far greater power, it must shake in its boots. It has no real Plan B.

It is surprising what the human brain does under oxygen deprivation. Yeled was shocked he had never asked the Royal Steward's name.

Dolos continued, sounding a bit more desperate now, like a career prosecuting attorney arguing another losing case. "Woman, this one's relationship to the King is now forfeit. He is *my* son. He agreed to my terms. Go ahead, ask him." He pointed arrogantly at the boy with his free hand. "The King's law, you see, is on my side. This pathetic boy is mine to do whatever I so desire."

Dolos smiled a most despicable smile and spit on the ground again.

Children, spitting is such a nasty habit. Don't do it. It's disrespectful and quite unsanitary. You are better than that. Back to the story.

Then, Noomai's eyes lit up like two grand, unquenchable bonfires, and her countenance inflamed like a great flaming star.

"You abominable deceiver. Isn't it enough you are allowed for a time to roam around the valleys and do your destruction? And yet you still seek to challenge the King and undermine his will. Have you never learned your place? Your arrogance is beyond measure. You have no authority here." Noomai flicked her hand like she was disposing of some nasty bug.

"This one is of the King and that will never change. Your claims are worth their weight in sheep dung. Release him now. Any delay is to your own peril."

Knowing once again he had fallen short and was defeated, Dolos snarled and released Yeled roughly. Yeled collapsed on the hard ground, gasping for air. Dolos, not daring to take his eyes off the Royal Steward, turned one last time to spit on the coughing Yeled.

"We are not done, you self-righteous witch," barked Dolos, pointing his white finger directly at her face—a pathetic final challenge of little weight at all. He was far outmatched and knew it. "You and I will have it out eventually. You'd best watch your back."

The Royal Steward just laughed out loud at the meaningless threat. She too was of the King and wielded his power. She relaxed a little, setting her arms gently at her side, and prophesied.

"Snake, in the end, you will wear out like a garment, like a thin, flimsy robe; you will just be rolled up and tossed like the rest of the trash into the fire and burned."

Yeled opened his eyes again, just in time to witness something remarkable, no, something miraculous. The Royal Steward rose on her tiptoes and reached up, grabbing the very corners of the world, and rolled it up like it was a beat-up old stage backdrop—Dolos, Apatê, the castle, the entire valley, the whole thing—and just kicked it aside.

Well, I didn't see that coming. Did you? Is this exciting, or what?

13

A Little Past Ouch

"Prince, Prince..." Yeled heard the voice again—a much kinder voice. It started off very quiet, as if it were from a great distance, but then grew louder.

"Prince, Prince, wake up; it is time to move on now."

When the prince awoke, he was back in bed—this time, sadly, a regular run-of-the-mill straw one. "Too bad," he thought. His head was still pounding, and though his wounds were dressed, his whole body ached horribly. His face was drenched with tears. So much had happened in a very short time.

The Royal Steward was shaking him, trying the best she could to wake him from his sleep. She was very concerned, of course. She had placed an immense number of smelly herbs, aromatic gooey salves and bandages on the prince's bites, cuts, scratches, whelps, abrasions, lacerations, gouges, scuffs, matted hair and, of course, many multicolored bruises. He winced at the fierce stink in the room and wondered if they were near a sewer. But soon, he realized the stink was him.

"Where am I?" His voice cracked. He was surprised to see he was still wearing his mangled, now blood-stained surcoat—or what was left of it—over what was left of his torn-up linen tunic.

"What happened?" he wondered to himself. His eyes shot around the room, looking for any clues. He even tried to get out of bed but was still too woozy to move. He could only sink back under the plain, rough wool comforter with a loud moan. His pillow, he noted, was far from superior.

Then the memories of recent days and events began seeping back into his recollection. There was the embarrassing confrontation with the Others, and then the horrific nightmare. But most of all, he remembered the incident with Dolos and the Royal Steward. Before he could say anything about it, the Royal Steward spoke.

"Welcome back to the land of the living, my prince, the beloved of the great King, the King's son."

"Where am I?" asked Yeled. "The last thing I remember was being in the castle of Lord Dolos—weeks there, in fact—and about to become his son. But then he changed... He wasn't kind at all. He was a..."

"Deceiver?" interrupted the Steward, nodding her head. "A snake? A liar? Yes, unfortunately, he was very real. I am sorry to say, not a dream—not like we think of dreams. Rather, maybe it is best to imagine him and his dark world as part of an alternate reality, where time and substance are out-of-sync with our reality—though still very destructive. In truth, you have been in this very bed for two days. I was very worried about you."

"Days!" exclaimed Yeled. "What do you mean? I was with Dolos for weeks."

"My prince, I have not left your side. I assure you. Your episode with the Others was only two days ago. It is confusing, but trust me, all will be revealed to those who are the King's."

The prince tried to get up but still felt a stabbing pain in his side.

"Please rest, my prince. You have bruised your ribs, maybe even fractured a few."

"Ah yes," Yeled nodded assent as he lay back on the hard pillow. "The beating from the Others. I suppose I messed up badly?"

"Yes, pretty much," said the steward, immediately nodding her assent, not in a judgmental way at all. "You didn't really stand a chance. Though you *were* quite valiant. After it was over, I flagged down a passing cart, and we got you to a nearby village and to this inn. You had a high fever for the first eight hours. I wondered if we would lose you. I was able to find local herbs and medicines at the market. I think you will be fine. Sorry for the smell, but you must take some time to heal."

"Time?" He asked, feeling some urgency now. He tried to get out of bed once more—will he never learn? Princes and princesses most often lack patience. I have researched it widely.

Though he tried, he only felt light-headed and had to lay back on his very unsatisfying straw pillow. "I had this crazy dream, a nightmare. My father was there; it was horrible, and when I saw his face, it wasn't his; it was mine. I don't understand. And then there was the Dolos thing. And you were there. You just rolled up the whole world as casually as someone would roll up a dusty rug. What... Who are you?"

The steward discerned it was time to explain some things to the prince. It was his quest, after all. He should begin to understand.

"Well, to start with, I too am concerned about your nightmare. There are deep-seated issues within you slowly robbing you of joy and hope. Trust is a very difficult thing for you. These issues are very powerful and so must be resolved by an even greater power. This too shall come to pass, more than you are aware.

"But Dolos? What is he all about?" said the prince, cutting her off as he frustratingly waved his arms in the air, suffering a stab of pain in his side for his troubles and his lack of patience.

"My prince," said the steward with great compassion. "I am sure I have said to you not all quests are the same. And truly, not all quests are what they seem."

That hardly helped. Yeled was even more confused but realized he needed to clear the air a bit.

"I have many questions but want to apologize to you, Steward. I have never even asked you your name. In fact, I don't know much about you at all. But what you did for me back there in the dark valley, and what you did to Dolos... It was...well... Who are you?"

The steward took a moment to gather her thoughts. She had known this conversation would eventually come. It was time.

"My name is Noomai. I have been with this King since the beginning of his reign. I proceeded from him with the charge to proclaim his character and nature to his people. I speak to any and all about his innate love for the unlovable, the unlovely, and the unloved."

"And to unlikely princes who fail their quests?" Yeled said with a nod.

"Especially them," Noomai said, smiling a most beautiful and endearing smile.

"So, Noomai, may I call you that?" She nodded kindly. "Who or what is Dolos?"

"It is a good question, my prince," said Noomai. "You know more than most who he is and what he is capable of. For a time, a little time, the serpent is allowed to roam the world and is made to be useful in the great King's larger, invisible plan. At some level, Dolos may even be aware he has limited freedom and even less time. He can go no further than he is allowed.

Such a vast irony. He is not only a powerful liar—in fact, there is none greater—yet he cannot even begin to see how crippled he is by his own disgusting lies. I assure you, he has no chance of defeating this King or his purposes, and since I go forth with the power of the King, he has no power over me either."

"So, are you saying he serves at the King's pleasure too?" asked Yeled with eyebrows furrowed.

"Yes, in a sense. He would never say so, of course. Yet all the kingdom serves this great King, whether they are aware of it or not, including snakes.

It comes back to the role of quests. All our journeys are made up of one quest after another. Each is ordained by the King for good. As you are beginning to see, no quest, including yours, is ever what it seems to be at the beginning. This King, your father, is without a doubt not what he appears."

"My quest?" asked Yeled, pausing. "Do I still have a quest?"

"Of course, my prince. But your quest," Noomai said, complete with air quotes, "will just have to wait a while. You are now officially on a quest-sabbatical."

Obviously, the last bit about the quest-sabbatical was totally made up, but it calmed the prince down some. It sounded legit to him.

"Oh, what difference does it make anyway?" The prince said, self-pity rising. "I have totally messed it up, haven't I? In the history of quests, this must be one of the worst." He looked away from the steward in shame.

Noomai smiled and said, "Yep, easily top five." She chuckled. When he realized she was joking, he smiled a little too. It really hurt. Then he chuckled, which hurt even more. Which made both laugh even more—which, well, you get the idea. They started giggling, chuckling, and laughing out loud with even a chortle or two, and each time the prince winced in pain, it started the whole guffawing thing over again.

The prince finally begged, "Oh, please, stop; don't make me laugh again. It hurts too much."

A couple of minutes of more-or-less silence passed.

"What am I going to do now?" he opined. "I only know how to be a prince—and a poor one at that. Am I to return to the Kingdom and face my father? Face his official disappointment and shame. Face the mocking from the people? From Nomos?"

"My prince," Noomai began with as much compassion and caring as anyone could muster. Gone was the frightening, larger-than-life façade Noomai had manifested in the presence of Dolos.

Now, she was humbly dressed in a comfortable white tunic. The prince guessed she had burned her gooed-up garment. She had also taken the blue ribbon from her hair, allowing her flowing white curls to drape softly over her thin, dark shoulders. Yeled noticed how attractive she was. He wondered what it would have been like if his mother were like her. Would he have turned out differently?

"My prince, no such thing will happen," she continued. "I will say to you once more, your father, the King, loves you with all the love in the Kingdom. He cannot love you any more or any less than he did before the quest. You cannot mess up such a love. I am certain of it."

"I want to thank you for your support and words of kindness, and for what you did to save me from Dolos—and myself, I suppose." The prince tried hard to say the right words to the steward, but he held no silly notion he would ever be welcomed back by this King—much less held in honor by him. The King was a great king and deserved a great son. He was just not *that* son. He had proven it.

But the steward is right about one thing. He must go and face the music, his last pathetic act as a prince.

After a few more days of rest and recovery, the two weary travelers hit the road again—this time on the long journey back to the castle. The prince was still embarrassingly dressed in what was left of his shredded surcoat on top of a thin linen tunic. He looked more like a beggar than a prince.

Noomai had done the best she could to clean up the coat of arms from the spider goo and sew up the surcoat where it was more or less respectable—at least at a distance.

But spider goo is nigh impossible to clean off. In fact, one industrious person was making bank marketing it as Flex Spider Goo. "Now you can fix your broken mead cup, mend your broken jewelry box, or even repair cracked arrows. Check it out; one drop of Flex Spider Goo can lift five dragons at once." The marketing was indeed impressive.

But I digress again. My bad. So much to say and so little time. The point is the prince still didn't look like a prince, and he surely didn't feel like one.

As they silently trudged step after step toward the Kingdom and, of course, the King, Yeled did what depressed people often do. He did a mental inventory of his life. His mind went all the way back to his childhood, long before the uprising in Garden City. Life was good then, he remembered, but he was just a child. Those times seemed good. Future bright. Everyone looked up to his mom and dad. Dolos had lied about that. Maybe they were a bit demanding. Or something else. Hmmm.

Then, things went badly. There was the coup and the poorly thought-out cavalry charge (he was willing to admit that now). There was the hurtful thing his dad said to him before the charge. "Boy, make your mother and me proud of you *this* time."

On their own, perhaps the last words were forgettable, but considering the following events, Yeled just kept repeating "this time" in his mind. "You mean there were other times?" His eyes furrowed together in some dismay as he thought about the significance. It sat in his head like a rotten piece of meat would sit in a stomach and make it turn over and over.

Did you know there is part of your brain where all your "ouches!" register? It's true. Whether you get bit by a spider, step on a rock, feel lonely, or if someone says something hurtful, there is a part of your brain designed to say, "Ouch!" Yeled's brain was saying 'ouch!' a lot, as much for the memory of the last words his father said as for the many owies he had suffered on the quest. And, he thought, his brain was also saying 'ouch!' for all the things his father didn't say, like "I am so proud of you, son!" You know.

He looked down at the dusty path in sadness. He wondered if he could only see his birth father again, would he ask what he meant? But alas, what a foolish thought. It can never happen. All he ever wanted to do was make his father proud of him. No judgment from me. All of us want to do the same thing.

Boys and girls, I will let you in on a little secret. Until that particular virulent "ouch!" was dealt with, Yeled still couldn't accept kind words from anyone, including the King. Even when the King said he was proud, Yeled couldn't process it. It's not all his fault. Dolos was not all wrong.

And here's the thing, and you, being a smart audience member, likely already figured this out. Quests are not designed to heal such wounds. They don't have the power.

This is where this particular special quest is spot on, and most other quest stories fall very short.

How many quest stories have you heard where the prince or princess goes out, fails to slay a dragon or two, falls into depression, wants to quit—but then solves the mysterious riddle of their coat of arms? It's an 'aha!' moment in the quest tale changing the royal's entire worldview. Using the secret of the coat of arms, he or she becomes a giant dragon slayer. Right? Then the moral of the typical quest tale is this: If you, like the prince, finally get the secret of the coat of arms riddle and can choose to incorporate it into your life, you too will become a great prince and live happily ever after—if you only do it enough.

Well, such things are just pulp fiction—run-of-the-mill quest tales, to be sure. Do you know what I mean?

We want to believe the knight would finally be successful, rise over their suffering if only they could figure out the secret of knighthood (the coat of arms), and boom, the "ouch!" would at last be healed.

Nope! Won't happen. Oh, don't get me wrong, it feels good to be regaled by a large audience for your accomplishments, to go on the vast quest-speaker circuit, to write "how to succeed in your quest" books—you know. But unresolved hurts will remain. They are deeply rooted and very powerful. It is even harder when, like Yeled and maybe you, there is no way to talk to the person who hurt you again. I am getting way ahead of myself, but there is one mysterious place where such a healing of secrets can take place. Ah, I have said too much for now.

Oh, I should also mention, we haven't said much about the coat of arms, have we? I promise you more is to come. It does hold mysteries, for sure—just not what you might expect.

"Oh, why did I push for this stupid quest?" said Yeled, berating himself one more time. It was easy for Yeled to criticize himself. Now, he must face the music.

The quest had, for all practical purposes, been grounded to an ignominious halt. They were limping home in disgrace. He had hoped there would be songs written about his victories and glory. Now he could only imagine the silly embarrassing songs written about him and *this* quest. Forever, he would be the unlikely prince.

Noomai knew better than to say much more at this point. She would have a moment soon. They had lost their rides, both horse and donkey, their supplies and their weapons. She purchased some dragon jerky and skins of water tiding them over, as long as they didn't run into any more dragons, spiders or gnomes. Or Others.

So, what do you do when you feel like it's time to give up?

A knight on his quest meets a wise teacher on the road as he is traveling. The man asks the teacher, "Which way to success?" The robed, bearded sage doesn't say anything. He just points into the distance.

The knight is thrilled by the prospect of finally experiencing success in his quest and runs off in the appointed direction. Suddenly, there comes a loud "Ouch!"

The knight limps back, a bit tattered, assuming he must have misinterpreted the message—and taken the wrong road.

He repeats his question, "Which way do I go to be successful?" Again, the counselor silently points the knight in the very same direction.

The knight shakes his head but obediently walks down the path once again. Maybe he did something wrong? Maybe he needed to have his sword out? Maybe the path is clear this time? It doesn't take long, once he is out of sight of the counselor, the air is filled with an even louder cry, "OUCH!" along with a deafening crushing sound and a spew of fire climbing the horizon.

When the bloody and charred knight crawls back to the feet of the sage, he angrily complains, "Twice, I asked you which is the way to success?" He swallowed hard and took a needed breath. "I did what you said, but I was crushed by the dragon of defeat, twice. This time, tell me the truth, old man."

Unmoved, the wise teacher compassionately looked down at the pathetic glory-seeking knight, and quietly said, "Success is that way. Just a little past 'Ouch!'"

14

Ye Wee Scunner

After they climbed a short rise, they could finally see the great King's castle, a long day's journey still.

The prince's emotions were roiling in his gut. Sure, he was relieved to be back, but he knew the next few days would be very painful for him.

"Castle Gazette Headline! '*The Unlikely Prince Comes Home After His Ugly Failed Quest,*'" Yeled imagined in his head. "But at least he salvaged his coat of arms—or at least bits and pieces of it!" he smirked as he looked down at the once-colorful crest, now just a carrier of hardened spider goo. The prince was depressed.

"Haud yer wheesht!" came a familiar voice from a patch of trees immediately off the road they were traveling. (That is Scottish for 'Just hold your tongue and listen!') It was Nomos. "Fit's 'at aboot?" (What's all that about?)

"Boy!" exclaimed the height-challenged Nomos as he lumbered toward the two travelers, his leather sandals slapping at each step. "I have bin lingering in this glade fur a long while to find out if the rumors are true. And listen, a nod's as guid as a wink tae a blind horse." (Meaning: explain yourself and make your meaning clear.)

Yeled couldn't help but smile at his former mentor. He had forgotten some of the Scottish-isms, but he was so glad to be in the safe company again.

"Well," Yeled began, with a broad smirk on his face, "to be sure, it's a dreich day!" Typically, this Scottish phrase refers to a miserable, cold, wet day in reference to the weather, but Yeled meant it more broadly. It referred to his very bad quest.

Then Nomos laughed out loud and warmly hugged Yeled for a long time. Nomos kissed the tearful Yeled on both cheeks.

"Aye, I missed you, you wee scunner!" exclaimed Nomos as he wiped a tear away from his bluish-grey eyes with his rough woolen shirt. (In Scottish, it means 'you little problem child'. Nomos meant it endearingly.)

Nomos' eyebrows were still full of shocks of white hair defying gravity and logic. Once, someone suggested he trim them. Nomos said he would miss such old and trusted friends.

"Tell me, lad, 'ow's the quest? Did you slay that nasty dragon?" Nomos asked, bringing up the elephant in the room.

"Nomos, with all due respect," opined Yeled. "I have failed badly. I have brought disgrace to myself and shame to my King. I am not worthy to be called his son."

Nomos paused for a while, not saying anything but compassionately gazing into the young lad's eyes. Then he spoke. "Oh, you foolish lad. Yer bum's oot the windae!" (Meaning: you're not making any sense.)

"You don't understand," Yeled said as subconscious defense mechanisms began to swell within him. "I failed the quest. I wrestled with many dragons, but..."

"Ah, lad, dinnae ya hear me. I didn't ask about *those* dragons. I could care less about those insignificant reptiles. I asked if you slayed *the* dragon. That was your quest, you see." Nomos paused and rubbed his full beard thoughtfully. What he said next was very unexpected.

"Laddie, may I have your permission to tell ye about yer mother and father?"

"My ma...my pa?" said a clearly confused Yeled. "Did you know them? I mean, were you in Garden City?"

"Aye, I knew them well," said Nomos. "None were closer, except the king, perhaps. Long before you came along, to be sure. There was a time..." Nomos said, almost drifting off, deep in thought. Tears formed in his eyes. He cleared his throat, wiped the tears away with his rough woolen overcoat, took a deep breath, and began again.

"Aye, there was a time when the two of them were something very special. None were more caring and compassionate. Your parents would do anything for anyone, especially the King. It was said they were the embodiment of the first two elements of your coat of arms, *mishpat* and *tzedakah*. They always put others first and then made things right if people were treated unjustly. They were filled with the spirit of the King like none before or after."

"But then, mysteriously, they turned; each inexplicably reached out and grabbed darkness instead of light. Some say, and I agree, they were tricked, but once the deed was done, they changed. They turned inward and self-focused—like frightened orphans who, at the end of the day, were desperately dependent on their own efforts and wiles to survive—no longer trusted anyone, especially the King."

"Wait," said Yeled. "Are you saying... wait, where was the King when all of this happened? Why didn't he step in?"

"Ah, no, it was they who abandoned the King. The King never abandoned them—not this king. They hid, not the other way around."

"And so, sadly, when ye came along," Nomos said, nodding his head and raising his bushy eyebrows for emphasis, "they had so little to give you. It's not all their fault, you see. You needed to see in their faces you were the most special child ever. You needed to hear again and again how wonderful you were and it didn't matter if you did this or that well, or well enough.

They couldn't give ya what you needed. They had lost it themselves. They were empty cups desperately trying to be filled any which way—well, except the one. But they were too proud, too ashamed or maybe too afraid—just too human—to look up into the adoring and forgiving gaze of the King again. They spent the rest of their tragic lives hidden away in Garden City."

"So," asked the prince in a rare moment of great clarity. "Are you saying I could never make my father proud of me? Not really?"

"Aye, that's the tragedy of it for you. Ya dinnae have that kind of power. Even the Royal Steward here can't do that. Yer ma and pa needed the King, but... there it is. Empty cups just can't fill other cups."

"Oh, my prince, to the point," said the Royal Steward with such spirit-empowered compassion. "What Nomos also means to say is quests can't heal those deep inner wounds. They are not designed to."

"Aye, ye scunner, ya see, yer quest isn't done yet—not near," said Nomos as he winked at the Royal Steward as if they shared a secret.

It turns out they did.

Nomos asked again, "Boy, tell me about your success with slaying *the* dragon."

Yeled was caught off guard. "Master Nomos, I would rather not go down that path again. It was, uh, a disaster. I could not have done worse."

"Balderdash!" exclaimed Nomos as he threw his stubby arms into the air. He spoke so loudly a flock of guineas erupted from a nearby ridge of grass.

"Boy, you dinnae hear the question right again. Will you tell me about *your* dragon? Those other beasties come and go. I'm talking aboot the *real* dragon."

The Royal Steward saw this as her cue and invited the confused Yeled to sit down on a nearby log. She put her arm on Yeled's left shoulder and slowly patted as if in rhythm with his heartbeat, calming him down and opening his mind to receive the truly good news he had never been able to hear before.

"My prince," the steward gently added, "you are, whether you know it or not, even though you never asked for it; you <u>are</u> a child of your father and mother. Inside your head is a hungry dragon voraciously consuming almost every compliment, every statement of love and every *so-be'd* honor. The beast quickly extinguishes any feelings of you being enough. Your dragon has been there for as long as you can remember and beyond, preventing you from feeling like the son any father would be proud of. So, the rest of your brain just kept working on feeding your beast. It's not all your fault. And so, your quest was ultimately designed for you to face that dragon—your dragon."

"I don't understand," exclaimed Yeled. "How can I slay a dragon I can't see? How can I slay a dragon that is in me? Is me?"

"Ya can't," said Nomos, interrupting as he placed one of his stubby fingers along the side of his nose to suggest, at last, the great secret was out. Nomos took out his long pipe. He had long given up smoking. It's bad for your health, you know. But it calmed him to put the unlit pipe in his mouth.

Then Nomos continued his thought. "That's the whole point—the irony of it all. Ya can't. You did all you could do, and it wasn't enough to even prick that dragon in ye. Now you have two paths left. You can keep feeding your inner dragon for the rest of your life. Good luck with that. You will never feel good enough. You will never feel your father is proud of you—enough."

"Or you can finally admit you can't do it and run helplessly to the arms of the King. There's real healing power there and there alone. Do what your parents wouldn't do—couldn't do. The choice is yours, lad."

The prince didn't know what to say. This was not what he was expecting. Is it true? If so, he'd lived his entire life chasing a lie or, worse yet, unknowingly trying to feed a hidden dragon whose hunger was unquenchable. Were they right?

"There's one more thing, my great prince," added the Royal Steward. "It's all been in your coat of arms."

You see, I told you we would get back to the coat of arms. Just not the way you were expecting. You'll be surprised, I think. Oh, back to the Royal Steward.

"My prince," said the steward, "at the very top is the victory of the King over that dragon, the very same one who tricked your parents. All else, *lipnay melek, mishpat* and *tzedakah,* are in the shadow of that great victory—you could say *sourced* by that lone victory."

"Now go to the very bottom. *Lipnay melek.* There is no path to becoming a great prince or princess where you don't run and throw yourself into the loving arms of the King over and over again. You must first be loved, honored and adored, and there is only one place where such a thing truly occurs. Isn't that what you've been longing for so long? Your parents were too proud or too afraid to submit to the King's great forgiveness and love. Until you experience *lipnay melek,* you have no power to really do *mishpat* or *tzedakah* anyway. You are too needy yourself to have anything to offer others."

"Empty cups can't be *mishpat* or *tzedakah.* Oh, they can try. They can go on quest after quest, but it is the *lipnay melek* of the King *alone* which can make one love others over oneself, even if it costs dearly. Your parents were *lipnay melek* until they weren't."

She went on. "So how do you gain this powerful healing spirit, the *lipnay melek*? To state the obvious, it is only accessed in the presence of the King, face to face, gaze to gaze, eye to eye, *lipnay melek.*"

"Empty cups will begin to be filled only as they hold empty hands upward in his arms. 'Father, I can't do this. Fill my cup and still my inner dragon a little or a lot today.' Truly great princes do this daily, for the dragon is never truly gone, only defeated daily by an even greater power."

"The key to experiencing what you have longed for all your life is not out here slaying this or that dragon or trying to prove yourself to Others. Do you want to feel truly good enough? Enoughness only happens *lipnay melek.*"

Instinctively, she wrapped her arms around his shoulders and hugged him close. "You are so loved, my prince. Far more than you can grasp at this moment. More than your inner dragon will let you, but you have never been closer to it. Breathe. Hear this, the voice of your King. 'You are my beloved son, with whom I am well pleased.'"

Nomos also had more to say. In fact, he was just warming up. He had waited a long time for this. Hardly fair.

"Prince, hear me well. It is lesser princes who look for honor in all the wrong places and end up settling for so much less, or nothing at all. They end up children of their parents, tragic empty cups."

"So, if I was so unprepared, then why was I sent on this quest?" The prince complained unprincely.

"Remember my prince? Ye requested it from the King. It was yer idea all along."

"The wink—of course!" thought the prince to himself.

"Irony again, ya left the presence of the King to find a putrid substitute for the presence of the King. But the further you went away, the worse ya felt. Simply put, the King knew ye would fail, humanly speaking. It was the goal of the quest, or at least the first level of the quest. Sometimes such shaming is a positive thing. In fact, redemptive shaming is a very good thing—or so I hear." He said the last part with a wink, a grin and a high jump where he clicked his heels.

"Even failure in the careful hands of a wise King can lead to an end far greater than all the successes of all time rolled into a single humongous ball. If, in yer failure, ye would come to see that ye are in greater need than ye have ever before imagined, it's all good. All ye ever needed was need, and ye dinnae have that until noo. And if the failure brings ya into his arms, what say ya?"

Nomos gave Yeled a toothy grin. He had practiced that line, and his delivery was flawless.

"Teacher, I am undone," Yeled uttered in a very reserved tone. "I sit here now, terrified to look into the eyes of the King, afraid of the reflection I will see. I couldn't stand rejection. I couldn't."

"Aye, remember, all ye need is need! Do ye have at least that? We will see. You can't avoid it. Your King and Father await your return."

Yeled shuddered noticeably. He wasn't sure about all he had just heard. He needed time to process, but he knew he needed to end this quest, no matter what.

15

Finale: The Great King

As the three travelers began to approach the royal city, a loud trumpet blew, ripping through the clear blue skies and interrupting the slight breeze. It was so loud it could be heard throughout the vast kingdom.

An armed entourage, mounted on great fiery steeds, exited the massive golden gates of the castle at full gallop. There were seventy-seven men and seventy-seven women—great warriors and heroes all. Each wore grand bronze helmets fitted with red plumes. Each carried body-length shields proudly portraying the great coat of arms. Each was fitted with fine, craftsman-made swords strapped to their waists.

Their splendor made Yeled feel so small and unimpressive. His shredded surcoat looked even more ragged and baggy as if his shoulders weren't wide enough to fill it.

The royal troop headed straight for the three exposed travelers. Yeled searched his mind for a word to describe the regal cavalcade. He landed on two—impressive and frightening.

In moments, the soldiers completely surrounded them. No matter which way you turned, there were tall horses standing in your way. They were snorting and swishing their long tails, scraping the dust with their hooves.

For your information, when horses are happy, they tend to snort. Not so for humans. That would be very awkward and off-putting. Not knowing much about horses, Yeled was feeling very exposed and threatened. Don't fret. I am not done with my tale. Okay, where was I? Oh yes, horses snorting, swishing, and scraping.

After a long pause, the western portion of the circle—the part closest to the castle gate—intentionally opened. Bright rays from the setting sun poured over Yeled, Nomos, and the Royal Steward. A new shadow appeared virtually blocking out the sun. It was the great King entering the circle. He was riding a pure black stallion so massive it made all others appear like mere ponies.

This was indeed a very great King.

"Prince..." roared the King, his voice echoing with seriousness and gravitas in the hollow formed by the circle of skilled warriors. His expression appeared quite solemn, even angry toward Yeled. His black eyebrows knit together severely. This is exactly what Yeled was afraid of—but also what he expected and knew he deserved.

"Prince," the King began again with a very grave and demanding tone. "How was your quest? Did you complete your charge? If I recall, you were told—by me..." The King put his finger to his lips and looked upwards as if saying this from memory.

"Thus, it was said, 'Every...EVERY aspect of the quest WILL be accomplished. There can be NO failure. You WILL find what you are looking for. No veering to the right or left, no hesitancy, no disappointment, for any negligence or dereliction at all would be quite consequential to you.'"

"Do you recall?" The King interrogated Yeled in a very off-putting loud voice. "This was the quest YOU requested—no more and no less. So, tell us about your travails. Tell us of your great, memorable battles. The great victories. Tell us about the honor you have earned. I wait. No, *we* wait." The King waved his arms around the armed soldiers. "Speak!"

The prince felt his pulse skyrocket, his legs felt wobbly and he worried he might throw up the jerky beginning to twist and turn in his warm stomach. He shrugged his shoulders and took a few shallow breaths. Then some more.

What could he say? He had no heroic tale—very few victories to speak of. This was going to be worse than he imagined. After a very long moment, during which the prince mainly looked at the ground, he began.

"Uh, great and mighty King...uh... Father...I...I didn't..."

"STOP!" yelled the Great King, cutting him off. Fierce royal eyes burned toward the hapless Yeled, and he quivered in trepidation. He had never heard the King so angry, so firm, so intense. This was quickly going downhill. At this moment, he had forgotten everything Nomos and the Royal Steward had told him.

The King shook his head in obvious disgust, his lips pursed and his expression dire. He swept his gaze across the circle of men and women, loyal warriors all. All eyes were upon the King, waiting for what he would say and do next.

Yeled was filled with apprehension and shame. Who wouldn't be? No judgment from me.

"Look, my faithful and trusted warriors," the King said as he pointed their attention to the nervous young man. "Behold my son, Yeled." He paused and even shook his head in disgust. This was indeed Yeled's worst nightmare.

Then the strangest thing happened. The King's face broke out into a huge royal smile. Then he laughed the greatest, deepest and most unexpected royal laugh ever laughed by any royalty anywhere before or since.

I have researched this thoroughly. There was a laugh by King Richard of Kent a decade or so ago when the Queen bore him triplets. Then there was the guffaw of the great Queen Simone after her army, made up entirely of women, had defeated another army made up of only men. As laughable as those laughs were, they were nowhere near—on the universal laughability scale—as laughter-rating as this King's laugh.

All his troops joined him, including Nomos and the Royal Steward. Everyone, except Yeled, was bent over in laughter. Only Yeled didn't get the joke, not yet anyway.

"BEHOLD!" the King proclaimed with a smile of great joy on his face as he pointed toward his confused and embarrassed son.

"See, my son, my beloved son, with whom I am well pleased and love more than love itself—he has returned from his holy quest. He has come into my presence, *lipnay melek* at last. I have missed him so much."

The Great King dismounted from his great steed and approached the prince with open arms. "Come into my arms, my son. Look up into my eyes and see how much I adore you as you are, not as you think you should be. I know what a great prince you will become. I am confident of it. But first, receive MY spirit, MY *mishpat,* and MY *tzedakah.* Your inner dragon is great, but it is no match for MY love."

The prince didn't wait until the King had finished his sentence. He threw himself into his kingly arms and wept. Never had he felt so welcomed, so honored, so valued. This...this is what he had been longing for—for so long.

After a few moments, the King raised his eyebrows and turned his head, feigning being critical. "What happened to the sword I gave you? And are those bee stings? I thought you hated bees. And what is that smell?" he grimaced a kingly grimace. "Spider goo?"

There was a wave of chuckling from the group—not critical at all. It was a chuckle from peers—a respectful chuckle. That is a very different thing. The King smiled openly and authentically at his bewildered son.

"Everyone, gaze upon him," the King proclaimed. "He is Sir Yeled, the rightful heir to the throne."

At this, the riders each dismounted, and to a person bowed to the ground in honor of the new knight of the realm, Sir Yeled.

Yeled couldn't breathe. This was not at all what he expected. He was struggling to make any sense of what just happened. One thing is for sure: this time, he felt something different.

After they all bowed, the soldiers circled Yeled, patted him on the back, and congratulated him on his new honor. This was a great thing; this was the highest level of recognition offered by the realm—apart from adoption, that is.

What happened, you ask? Well, if you've been listening to the tale, you should know the nature of this King and his love by now. The King's love for his son cannot be stronger; it cannot be diminished. It didn't need a quest, successful or not, to be proven or earned.

In Yeled's defense, how could he have known about such love before his adoption? He hadn't received anything close from his biological father or mother, to be sure. Only this Great King's love is, by nature, so loving.

"My beloved son, Prince Yeled," said the King with a voice so warm and endearing, sounding more like the Royal Steward than Nomos. "Welcome home. My castle is just not the same without you. Now you know the mysteries of my love. My love is for the unlovable, the unlovely, the unloved, the undesired, and the undesirable. It is even for those who, like so many, feel like disappointments to their fathers and mothers. I love failed princes and princesses. That's all there is."

"And failed stewards," said the Royal Steward a bit sheepishly, though with a smile.

"And failed viziers as well," winked Nomos with a Scottish dance of some sort.

"Look around you," added the King. "See the dozen-dozen warriors who now embrace you? Like you, some of them were also orphaned; some were addicts, homeless, riddled with unforgiveness or just angry at the world. Some were rebels and bullies themselves; others hated me and what I stood for. That's where I found them."

"The same dragon in their brains had devoured any sense of worth, honor or being desired or desirable. Each first needed healing through my love and my embrace. Some were even more stubborn than you. Is that even possible? There is only one power greater than such a dragon. The experience of my love in my presence *lipnay melek*, is the only power able to even begin to slay their own inner dragon."

"Now you see the goal of your quest wasn't for you to succeed or earn my love. You really must hear some of the hilarious stories from these other men and women who went on their own quests with very similar outcomes.

A couple of them had to fight flocks of relentless, crazed chickens. Others had to deal with endless computer spam messages that some total stranger in a faraway country across the ocean had left his entire estate of $1,232,500 to you as long as you sent them your Social Security Number. Very tricky, indeed. No one had done well when confronted with Others."

"They each failed miserably too." The King paused and grinned. "Not as badly as you, my son. To be sure, you have set a new bar." The group of soldiers all shared a laugh. Yeled chuckled too. He was not offended; in fact, he felt only respect from his peers. His dragon had been stilled for now.

"No," the King continued with a joyful heart. "The purpose of the quest was for you to begin to see your problem wasn't what has or hasn't happened to you in your life, your successes or failures, the amount of love showered upon you or not by your parents. It was solely designed to expose a hidden internal enemy preventing you from feeling *any* honor or love. You already had my love but couldn't receive it. You are not alone."

"All I need is need..." Yeled remembered being told repeatedly by both Nomos and the Royal Steward.

"Be wary," said the King. "Your dragon is only <u>mostly</u> slain, my son. It will rise again and again. You will learn to regularly access my powerful love in my presence. I will make it so."

"Now, having said that," the King chuckled. "Still, we do need to work on you becoming a better warrior. And of course, we need to get you another sword. Maybe you will get another shot at those slimy beasts soon."

"But not now. We have a banquet prepared in your honor so the entire Kingdom can see you in all your splendor. Sir Yeled, the prince and heir to the throne. Oh yes, but before the grand banquet, my formerly hygienic son, you really do need a long hot bath."

The King kissed Yeled on both cheeks and then hugged him again. Yeled's heart was filled with such joy, such relief and such a feeling of being enough—more than he could ever remember feeling. He was the prince, the beloved of the King, *lipnay melek* at last.

The warriors' voices rang out with the tri-part acclamation reserved for great victors after great victories. "Huzzah for Sir Yeled. Huzzah, huzzah!"

"Let it be known and proclaimed," said the Royal Steward. "This Great King loves unlikely princes and princesses. That's all there is. In his presence, they become great. They become *mishpat* and *tzedakah*."

16

One Tale's End Is Another's Beginning

Berenice took a deep breath, looked up at the audience, and graciously shut the leather book, proclaiming with a broad, endearing smile, "It is finished!"

"Thank you for listening to my tale. May I say one more thing, if you would allow me? I do not want to overstep my welcome, but it must be said. I have said it before. That nasty inner dragon, shame, is very powerful and natural to all human beings, and certainly so for princes and princesses. It arrives very young and is felt every time you get beat up by nasty dragons, spiders, bees or when you are bullied by the Others and truth be told, your own mirror.

The inner dragon of shame has great power to make you feel unlovable and unworthy of any honor by mommies or daddies. It can make you afraid to look into the King's eyes—afraid of seeing his disgust— or worse, his rejection.

Yet the truth is so much bigger than your errant, all-too-human feelings. All the time the prince was on this quest, the King never stopped loving him. It is right to say the King loved Yeled even more than Yeled loved himself. But because something was broken inside him, Yeled couldn't feel love and honor until the love of the King manifested something new.

This is where the King found Yeled, but he did not leave him there. It is rightly said the King is making all things new.

Can you hear this King's voice too? "My son, my daughter, I am so proud of you. I am your biggest supporter and fan. I will always have your back. I love you as much as I did before. You have not failed—not in my eyes. You can't. You are my son, my daughter. You cannot add to that assessment. You cannot take anything away from it. My love for you and my sense of your worth were never dependent upon whatever success you may or may not have had. You are my son, my daughter. I can't love you any more or less than I do now. The King remains, making all things new. The End!"

After the Royal Storyteller, Berenice said, "The End," there was a long, pregnant pause, no one breathed, and a warm stillness and quiet blossomed throughout the auditorium. No one moved either. Clearly, no one wanted the evening to be over. It all went so quickly—too quickly. It was wonderful.

Then one brave person stood and began to clap, then another, and another, and before long, the hall erupted into a massive standing ovation.

Some moved toward the high stage to thank Berenice personally and maybe get a selfie with her. Others remained in their rows, just drinking in the special scene. Some men, in particular, were visibly moved and had to be consoled by their partners and spouses. They understood it in a special way. Surely the King's work was being done throughout this wonderful night. People had changed. That's what good stories can do.

But then it happened.

Suddenly, grey shadows appeared on the high, domed glass roof arching high over the stage. If the crowd had been quieter, you would have been able to hear the faint sound of footsteps echo through the night. These mysterious masked people had chosen the roof as their entry point, utilizing their skills in stealth and agility. They were clad in weathered, tattered garments, adorned with weapons gleaming in the moonlight. The first thing anyone noticed was a powerful explosion ripping through the glass dome. Shattered glass showered upon everyone as men, women, boys and girls ran for cover.

It was unbelievable, unimaginable and incomprehensible! A violation of everything marking a truly civilized society. This is not to say there was no crime in the kingdom or everyone treated everyone else with kindness and equality. There was indeed a hodgepodge of ruffians, hooligans, bullies and thugs. There were pirates and pirate ships freely roaming the distant seas of the Kingdom, disrupting shipping and commerce illegally. The King's troops had long attempted to end their chaos but with little luck.

Nothing this brash, crazy or invasive has ever occurred in anyone's memory.

Without missing a beat, at the edge of the roof, the scoundrels secured sturdy ropes to multiple anchor points. These ropes were thick and well-worn, likely having endured countless adventures and daring escapes. Each brute fastened a harness around their waist, attaching it securely to the rope. One by one, they stepped onto the edge of the ceiling, their hearts pounding with anticipation. With calculated movements, they leaned back, placing their trust in the ropes supporting them. Quickly, they began to descend, using their hands to grip the rope and their feet to control their descent. As they repelled down, the masked invaders showed remarkable dexterity and fearlessness, effortlessly maneuvering their way along the rope. Their movements were fluid and precise, betraying years of experience and a close affinity for such clandestine affairs.

They were clearly professionals and they knew exactly what their dark assignment was tonight. They approached the ground with a controlled descent, their boots touching the stage with a soft thud—never taking their eyes off their surprised single target.

Two of the larger assailants roughly grabbed Berenice, put a dark hood over her head and then disappeared the very same way they came. All of this happened so quickly no one moved to stop it. What could they have done anyway? Even the King's trained guards were caught totally flat-footed.

Surely, the evening went from exhilaration to shock and despair in only a few moments.

What happened? Now what was to be done?

The King would launch an immediate investigation and a rescue, but how and where? The next day, there was no sign of the assailants anywhere. There were no eyewitnesses, no trail. The King sent soldiers to the port to see if there was any evidence of pirates or pirate ships. No one had seen hide nor hair of anything resembling buccaneers, raiders or cutthroats of any kind. As of today, there has been no ransom request and no explanation. It is a mystery.

Don't be alarmed. We will not leave Berenice without aid. She has already had to deal with so much tragedy and trauma in her life. She is a miracle. This must be resolved, and Berenice must be brought home quickly and without harm. But how? Have no doubt. There is so much more to come.

Don't miss the next book in our Kingdom Quest series, *The Storyteller's Tale.*

17

post·lude | \ 'pōst-ˌlüd

A postlude is music played after a musical program has concluded. It's most often heard after sacred, religious or ceremonial meetings, such as worship services. The music is intended to continue the feeling of the meeting as the attendees re-enter their day-to-day lives.

So, let the now-familiar concluding music begin.

So, in our tale, did everyone live "happily ever after"? No, of course not. That's a Disney fairy tale. The story of the "Tale of the Unlikely Prince" is anything but that.

Yeled, uh... Sir Yeled has now returned to the Royal Castle and into the loving arms of the King (*lipnay melek*). Yet he continues to struggle with the unimaginably wonderful and inexplicable love of the King for him as he is. That inner dragon has been neutered a bit, but not completely.

There are moments, though, when he is truly swept up in the glory of the King's adoration and love. There are now times when he truly feels that the King is his biggest fan and supporter. He has come to know that the King will always have his back—even after wildly miserable quests, which he continues to have. Usually, these times are when he enjoys an intimate, intentional audience with the Great King. More and more, he is beginning to look up into the Great King's measuring gaze. He couldn't do that before the quest. He had too many negative thoughts running through his mind. Truly, it is not all his fault.

In those precious moments, which do seem to be happening more often lately, he feels humbled, honored, enough and even princely. He is now the 'grateful' prince. Maybe a good word is 'enviable.'

But then, at other times, he can fall into a dark frump where he starts to wonder if the King is impatient with his slow maturation and warrior-ness. "Surely the King would prefer—and even deserves a better son who could defeat more dragons, yes?" says that inner critical voice over and over, particularly after a bad training day with Nomos.

He is not alone. It is my observation that this is a constant daily struggle for all great princes and princesses, to be sure.

One thing has changed. We see Sir Yeled seeking the counsel of the Royal Steward more and more, requesting that she assist him in experiencing the King's love more. He lets her words wash over him again and again. It is as if she is speaking directly to his inner dragon, and it is making a difference. He is learning through her wisdom and counsel, of course. But there is also some kind of mysterious power to her words, effervescing within them, that seems to make him trust the King's love for him more—a little more anyway.

He has learned a very important lesson. Princes don't have this kind of trust, not normally. This kind of trust can only come from being *lipnay melek*. It is sourced from the royal vaults alone and is not innate to princes or princesses. Princes and princesses just don't have that muscle group, no matter how hard they try. It is born from the heart of the Great King. Princes must ask for it and receive it with empty hands. Daily, *lipnay melek*.

How does one know? He or she begins to prioritize *mishpat* and *tzedakah*, a wonderful other orientation that is noticeable in an increasingly indifferent and selfish world.

The core truth of our tale? The King does not love the worthy. It is the King's love that makes one worthy.

It appears that the quest continues.

www.ingramcontent.com/pod-product-compliance
Lightning Source LLC
Chambersburg PA
CBHW061545310726
48972CB00008B/2612